MY WIFE'S LOVER

This new collection d's foremost practitioners is remarkable for its ran al-documentary to the outlandishly surreal; from the comic and satirical to the uncanny and disturbing.

With his customary playful inventiveness, Herdman moves lightly from the moral equivocations of a desperate literary biographer, in pursuit of a *femme fatale*, to the sad case of a heretical clergyman who goes on fire during a country church service; from the nostalgic memories of an ageing Scottish Nationalist to social-class farce and mayhem on a luxury-cruise liner.

But all this diversity is held together by the author's highly individual style and by his underlying thematic pre-occupation with perennial questions of truth and delusion. Thus, the stories presented in this volume continue the dark exploration of ambiguous worlds familiar to readers of *Imelda*, *Ghostwriting*, and *The Sinister Cabaret*. Those three earlier novels are also available from:

www.blackacebooks.com

JOHN HERDMAN

The author was born in Edinburgh in 1941 and now lives in Highland Perthshire. Fuller biographical details and a critical appreciation can be found in Macdonald Daly's Introduction to Herdman's *Four Tales*, Zoilus Press, 2000. The author's own web site is:

www.johnherdman.co.uk

by the same author

fiction

Descent

A Truth Lover

Memoirs of my Aunt Minnie / Clapperton

Pagan's Pilgrimage

Stories Short and Tall

Imelda and Other Stories

Ghostwriting

Four Tales

The Sinister Cabaret

drama

Cruising

non-fiction

Voice Without Restraint:
Bob Dylan's Lyrics and their Background

The Double in Nineteenth-Century Fiction

Poets, Pubs, Polls & Pillar Boxes

To Isobel + Bob
with warmest good wishes
from John.
27:xii:06.

My Wife's Lovers

ten tales

John Herdman

John Herdman.

BLACK ACE BOOKS

First published in 2007 by Black Ace Books
PO Box 7547, Perth, PH2 1AU, Scotland

www.blackacebooks.com

Typeset in Scotland by Black Ace Editorial

Printed in England by CPI Antony Rowe
Bumper's Farm, Chippenham, Wiltshire, SN14 6LH

A CIP catalogue record for this book
is available from the British Library

ISBN 978–187298877–1

ACKNOWLEDGEMENTS

The title story was first published in *Fras*. 'The Blazing Curate', 'The Owl of Soilluc' and 'Plaintiff' were also first published by Fras Publications as a pamphlet entitled *Triptych*. The story 'Cruising' is based on the author's play of the same title, which was published by diehard. The poem towards the end of 'Aldengrave the Alchemist' was first published, under the title 'Snawed Up', in Scotia in 1971. 'Monkey Tricks', under the title 'The Monkey', first appeared in *The London Magazine*.

The verse from Kenneth White's poem 'What Enid Starkie Didn't Know', quoted in 'Voyaging', is reproduced from *Open World: The Collected Poems 1960–2000* by kind permission both of Kenneth White and his publisher, Polygon, an imprint of Birlinn Ltd.

The coda verse by Bankei Yotaku was found at an Internet posting without a translation credit. If the translation is in copyright then the present author and publisher wish to record their debt of gratitude to the translator and his or her publisher.

The author acknowledges support from the Scottish Arts Council towards the writing of the stories which make up this volume.

For Mary

On a huge hill,
Cragged, and steep, Truth stands, and hee that will
Reach her, about must, and about must goe;
And what the hills suddennes resists, winne so;
Yet strive so, that before age, deaths twilight,
Thy Soule rest, for none can worke in that night.

John Donne, Satyre III

CONTENTS

1	My Wife's Lovers	11
2	The Blazing Curate	37
3	The Owl of Soilluc	49
4	Death and Devolution	61
5	Voyaging	79
6	Cruising	95
7	Aldengrave the Alchemist	125
8	Plaintiff	137
9	Monkey Tricks	153
10	Tom na Croiche	161

1

My Wife's Lovers

Dear Mr Duffus,

The news of your wife's death came as a peculiar kind of shock to me. It's not shocking that she should have died, of course, because she was old; not exceptionally so by today's standards of female longevity, it's true, but certainly of a very good age. So when I say (as I do) that the sort of shock I felt was one which contains an admixture of satisfaction, you will understand that I am not being spiteful: everyone has to die eventually, and it's not as if I can be glad that she was taken before her time, or anything as petty as that. More a feeling of *consummatum est*, perhaps – a 'well, that's finished at last'. Maybe that's what I'm feeling.

Why 'shock' at all, then? Is that really the *mot juste*?

Yes, I believe it is.

For when one has known someone as intimately as I knew your late wife, the realization that she has ceased, *tout court*, to exist, is always and in the strictest sense shocking. To think that those limbs once so straight and proud, that glorious, light-bespangled hair, that skin so whitely delicate and silky on the inside of the thigh – I could go on, but this is neither the time nor the place. That they have ceased to be, in short. Even though, for a very long time now, no longer quite what they were, to say the least – now altogether gone. Not even food for worms, but actually incinerated. Yes, that is shocking. Notwithstanding that she was the instrument, willing or unwilling, of one's torment.

I hope, Mr Duffus, that she was never the instrument of yours. (I trust that doesn't sound patronizing.) Oh, I know that at one time, long ago, she must have been so. But I have heard that after she married you she did eventually 'settle down', as they say; domesticity and late motherhood did their usual sterling work to that effect. It does seem unlikely, I know, given her track record, but . . . anyway, *de mortuis*, etc. Now is not the time to rake up all that old muck. Such is far from my intention. I have no wish to say anything inappropriate to an occasion such as this.

Anyway, what I started off to say – my sympathy, Mr Duffus. Forgive an old fool for rambling on so irrelevantly. My deep and genuine sympathy. It would not do to forget that.

Yours very sincerely,
An old friend of Kathleen's

The old hand trembled slightly as he took the letter back from mine, but as he replaced it beneath the little figure of Sir William Younger which served as a paperweight on his desk he looked me straight in the eye. In his own the hint of a tear glistened, and I looked down respectfully. A courageous old chap, I thought, succeeding beyond reasonable expectation in maintaining his dignity in what could only be described as trying circumstances.

'I don't suppose you can shed any light on that, Dr Halliday?'

I shook my head. 'I'm afraid not, Mr Duffus. I'm as much in the dark as you – maybe even more so. Your late wife's name was given to me as being, just possibly – and if I had identified her correctly from the information given me – the mysterious person with whom the subject of my book had been in some way . . . involved, during a crucial period of his youth. And who became, I suppose you could say, his Muse. That's all, really. As to the background, the general ambience, I don't know a great deal as yet, and as far as your wife's possible rôle . . . '

My voice trailed off. This was embarrassing for both of us.

Let me explain. I am a professional biographer, and I am writing the life of the Scottish novelist Alexander Buchanan, 1915–79. The great Scottish novelist, as some would have it. But that is not for myself to judge, I believe. Certainly he was an extraordinary one. I am not of the school of the 'critical biographer': I never make any attempt to analyse or evaluate the work. That is the job of others and I leave it to them. My part is to chronicle; and I pride myself on being a bit of a sleuth. Not that there weren't a few academics who were furious that I had landed this job. I myself have no academic post, you see; I have always spurned all that. There were those who cheekily suggested, I've been told, that I was chosen because I had insinuated myself into the good graces of the writer's widow. There are even some who accuse us of immoral relations; but I do not wish to trouble to give the lie to such calumnies – as someone else once said in a rather different context. Nathalie Buchanan was fifteen years the novelist's junior and about the same amount older than myself. I met her at a memorial event for Buchanan, actually, to mark the tenth anniversary of his death. An attractive and well preserved lady of French extraction. She stood up and made a speech. When a widow, on such an occasion, gets up and starts her piece with the words 'Sandy Buchanan was not an easy man . . . ' you know that he must have been a very difficult man indeed. The concessive clauses followed, as one might expect, and filled up most of the remainder of the address, but the initial impression was indelible. I confess I was intrigued.

I introduced myself to Nathalie at the end of the official part of the evening and asked her a few questions, in a conversational manner appropriate to the occasion: probing, yes, but not too deeply or insistently, and I think with a good deal of tact. I believe she found me impressive, and perhaps even charming, but no more than that. I asked her whether any biography had yet been contracted; none had, though there had been approaches, to none of which Nathalie had felt inclined to respond positively. We agreed to meet the following week; and in a surprisingly short time an agreement had been reached. I think we both felt that we understood each other. I found Nathalie responsive and at the same time responsible – and, for her part, I believe she instinctively trusted me.

The initial spade-work was straightforward enough, and since I had Nathalie's full co-operation the early years of Buchanan's life fell to me easily. His ancestry, his childhood in Aberdeen, the son of a well-to-do lawyer, his distinguished schooldays – there was plenty of documentation for all of this, and many reminiscences of friends and contemporaries recorded during his lifetime and immediately after it, in the years since he had achieved a measure of fame. And for most aspects of his life in Edinburgh, from the time he went to the university until he left for the war, there was no lack of sources. These included a plentiful supply of people ready and even anxious to talk about him, even though very many of his own generation had regrettably now passed from the scene. There was only one objective in pursuit of which I unfailingly, and always swiftly, came up against a brick wall, and that was the very crux which for any biographer of Buchanan had to be pivotal – the identity of 'Rosalind'.

Readers of Buchanan will be aware that it is around this mysterious figure that his first major work, *First Class Single to Nowhere* (1949), revolves: circling and approaching, retreating and returning and never reaching. It is not a matter of the protagonist failing to attain her, though whether or in what sense he does attain her remains teasingly elusive; it is rather the reader who never 'reaches' Rosalind – that is the astonishing originality of the novel's concept. That is, Rosalind fails to appear in the narrative at all; in person, I mean. She is not directly portrayed, but her presence is summoned up by the conversations and passing references of others, through the skilful evocation of the ambient context, and of course by the internal musings and the bizarre actions of the protagonist, Stoddart.

That Stoddart is transparently the young Buchanan is what makes the identification of Rosalind a biographical imperative. Buchanan wrote the work in Paris in the years following his war service in Burma, an experience of which he always refused to speak but which many critics consider the crucial submerged fact underlying all his later writing. His equal secretiveness about Rosalind and about Burma has led some to suggest that the former was never a real person at all, but instead symbolized or constellated something (exactly what, these critics are never able to say) which happened to him during the war years. But I do not believe that at all.

There was certainly at one time a handful of people to whom, in strictest secrecy, Buchanan had confided the identity of Rosalind, or who were otherwise aware of it. There is unimpeachable evidence of that. But unfortunately these people are all dead, nor did any of them pass the secret on during their lifetimes. It is a measure of the force of the novelist's personality, of the loyalty he inspired and also his judgment of character, that these beans were never spilt. And crucially, Buchanan had never confided this information to Nathalie. He had not married her until 1960, two decades after the events on which his novel was apparently based were over and done with, and he had never spoken to her about them. For her own part, she had naturally felt inhibited and quite uninclined to raise the matter; and probably, if the truth were known, preferred to remain in ignorance.

But after pursuing what seemed every possible lead in vain, getting absolutely nowhere and becoming quite depressed at the prospect of publishing a biography with an aching void at its very centre, I quite unexpectedly had one of those breakthroughs which do sometimes come the way of those in my profession, and always gladden the heart. I happened to meet up, about another matter altogether, with a minor literary figure whom it had not even occurred to me to interview in this connection, as although he had known Buchanan as an admirer and something of an acolyte of the novelist, he was half a generation younger and not the sort whom a man like Buchanan would ever have dreamt of making a confidant. A sleek but ageing little man with a tired face and a tense jaw. But when I mentioned to him casually what I was working on, and the difficulty I had come up against, he was immediately on the alert. He glanced up at me quickly from his drink, an almost furtive look in his eye.

'I can give you a name,' he said.

Now this man needed something from me, which was why he had asked to meet me, and it was something, as it happened, that I didn't feel over-inclined to give him. This was clearly his golden opportunity to wrest it from me, and the price was his information. But I wasn't going to buy until I had good reason to suppose that the goods were genuine.

'Tell me first of all how you know it,' I responded.

'I will. When I first came to Edinburgh as a student there was a folk club I used to go to. It was mostly students who went, but sometimes older folk would go along too. One time I was in the company of a couple of these older women, and they started talking about a girl who had enjoyed a certain notoriety in the years before the war. She had moved in a "bohemian set", apparently – that sort of thing. They spoke a bit about her, the things she got up to. Yes, they mentioned her name. I wasn't paying a great deal of attention – it didn't interest me, particularly. Then one of them said, "She was Sandy Buchanan's 'Rosalind', of course." "Really?" said the other. "I didn't know that." "Oh, there's no doubt about it." The second one asked what had become of her, and the first said, "Oh, she went away a long time ago." That was it. But I did take care to store the name in my memory.'

I looked at my informant shrewdly. The very sketchiness of the story seemed to me suggestive. The man had run it off without any appearance of hesitation or improvisation – and there were no little details put in for the sake of verisimilitude. In retrospect I am inclined to think that he knew all along that I was on the trail of Rosalind, and had realized his opportunity – that was why he had asked to meet up with me at this point. At any rate, I decided that I didn't have a great deal to risk except making a fool of myself, and I've often enough done that in the course of my career.

'So what was the name?'

My companion smiled knowingly, aware that he had got what he was after.

'The name', he said with teasing slowness, 'was Kathleen Caldwell.'

After that, things went for a time almost ridiculously easily. Although it is never explicitly stated in *First Class Single to Nowhere*, the probability seemed to be that 'Rosalind' had been a student around the same time as Stoddart. The university handbooks for the relevant years were the obvious starting-point, and they indeed revealed that a Kathleen Macpherson Caldwell had graduated in modern languages in 1936, the year before Buchanan had graduated in history. I then turned to the annual register of graduates, and discovered that her home address (which remained constant until her marriage, though probably she spent little time there) was in Brechin. For the next few years her occupation is given as 'art student', which eventually gives way to 'art teacher'. In 1947 the former Miss Caldwell becomes Mrs Duffus, with an address in Montrose. A visit to West Register House was next on my agenda. This yielded her birth certificate, showing that she was born on 5 June 1914, the daughter of James Caldwell, bank clerk, and Euphemia Caldwell, maiden surname Cruikshank. By the time she marries Roderick John Duffus, teacher, on 16 July 1947, her father has become a bank manager and her mother has died. Thereafter she continues to live in Montrose, changing her address only once. Finally – and this was almost too good to be true – a quick check of the most recent available electoral roll showed that, just under a year previously, Roderick J. Duffus and Kathleen M. Duffus were both still alive, registered to vote, and living at the same address in Montrose.

By this time I had built up in my mind a sense of the likely trajectory of Kathleen's life. In my trade one develops an instinct for this kind of thing. A young girl from a respectable and restricted small-town background wins a place at the university. She goes off to the big city, and the sense of liberation is immense. She dabbles in the arts and mixes with what in those days used to be called a 'fast set'. She is vivacious and charismatic, and of course highly attractive to men. 'Free love' and other such 'modern' ideas are naturally in the air, but there is something private and elusive about her which enhances her attraction and at the same time inhibits the more sensitive and inward of her admirers. In short she is cut out to be a *femme fatale*, and the object of what Jung would call a 'negative anima projection'. That is clearly the rôle which she plays for Buchanan.

But after some years of this kind of life she begins to become weary. She is slowly sickened by her own inconstancies, her minor deceptions and cruelties. Perhaps – and this is the most likely thing – someone has come along who has deeply engaged her own emotions and done to her what she has so often and so thoughtlessly done to others. Her lack of self-esteem, hitherto so well hidden under a confident and extravert exterior, comes to the surface and she realizes that she hates and despises herself. With an impetuous movement of the will she decides to throw in her present life and return to her home town. Perhaps it is her intention at first to stay for only a short time while she recovers her emotional equilibrium. But she is sucked back into this life which is so much stronger than her, so much more really a part of herself than the superficial life she has been living in Edinburgh, though she doesn't clearly know it. She meets a nice local man – perhaps he is someone she has known all her life and who has always held a candle for her, but whom up to now she has tended, in his very familiarity, affectionately to despise. But she is weary, and he is kind and supportive. He wants her to marry him. Well, why not, after all?

She doesn't love him, perhaps. But everything that really matters to her, she tells herself, is behind her. Nothing is going to bring back Mr X who has betrayed her, and so on. And she wants to have children before it is too late . . .

Yes, that's the way it must have been, or something very like it. And she does marry and settle down. And have a child. And is happy and contented, after a fashion.

Well, and she is still alive, and perhaps available for interview! Will she want to talk about the past? Is she ashamed of her treatment of Buchanan as so subtly and intricately implied in that wretched novel? Will she want to deny it all, claim that Rosalind was someone else, or pretend that none of it had ever happened? Or, on the contrary, will she welcome the chance to put the record straight and give her own side of the picture?

There was only one way to find out. The prospect of meeting her made me rather nervous, I confess, but I determined to write to her. The letter was very straightforward and most tactful. I said simply that I was writing the biography of Alexander Buchanan and had heard that she might have known him in his youth. There were few of his generation still living, and naturally if she could furnish me with any recollections at all, however sparse they might seem, that would be of the greatest help to me in my work. If, however, the information I had received was wrong or if she was not the person I thought she was – or, indeed, if she simply did not wish to discuss Alexander Buchanan or her possible friendship with him – then that would be the end of the matter and she would hear no more about it. I thanked her in advance but also apologized for the intrusion. With a little trepidation but also with a undeniable sense of excitement, I addressed the envelope and dropped it in the pillar box.

I heard nothing for three weeks. Then I received a

phone call from Mr Duffus, with shocking news. He had found his wife Kathleen sitting dead in her chair one morning, from what proved to be a massive heart attack, with my recently opened letter beside her on the table. You can imagine what I felt. Completely taken aback, I could only mumble my sympathy. But Mr Duffus seemed unresentful, and, though clearly suffering, in control of his emotions. He wanted to know what lay behind my letter so that he could put himself in the picture and come to terms with whatever he had to. Alexander Buchanan was only a name to him, he said, and he had read none of his books, but it appeared his wife had had some connection with the novelist which he would be interested to learn more of. Would I be willing to come and see him? Of course I would, of course. A date was fixed for the following week, and I drove up to Montrose on a bleak and bitter day in early March.

'Who on earth would write such a letter?' Mr Duffus asked wistfully, not as if expecting an answer. He gazed out of the sitting-room window, which looked out to the west, in the direction of Brechin where he had met his wife half a century earlier. She had come there as an art teacher at the high school, he explained, where he himself had already been teaching for several years. They had fallen for each other almost at once.

'And now, to learn something like this – after all these years. One knew, naturally, that she had had a life before she met me – nobody in their thirties has an emotional clean slate, so to speak . . . but that she should have a past haunting enough to kill her, or so it would seem, and that I never had so much as a hint of it – that's a bit hard to come to terms with.' The dignified old man was struggling to control his emotions.

'Perhaps you shouldn't make too much of this horrible letter,' I offered lamely. 'It reads to me as if written by someone twisted, motivated by spite.'

'Spite, yes – but why? That's the question.'

I couldn't answer him. The 'letter of sympathy', if it could be called that, had reached Mr Duffus only the previous day, well after our meeting had been arranged, so he had not mentioned it to me before my arrival that morning.

'Besides,' he added, with a sudden sharp look at me, 'it wasn't this letter which killed Kathleen. It was yours.'

This cut me to the quick. Though obviously nothing could have been further from my intention, it did look as if my carefully constructed little missive, which I had thought so tactful and considerate, had made a fatal impact upon Mrs Duffus. Sorry though I was that it had had this consequence – desperately sorry, and not only because it made my own task so much harder – I couldn't help, as a biographer, feeling excited about what it implied. What could there conceivably have been in this woman's past, in her relationship with my subject, that the mere possibility of its exposure should produce such a devastating effect? True, much was already implied in the novel, but even so . . .

All that was whirling about in my head and horribly mixed up with an involuntary sense of shame, and I looked at the floor, avoiding Mr Duffus's eye, once again unable to make a reply.

'I know, I know,' said the old man impulsively, and laying a sympathetic hand on my arm. 'You couldn't have foreseen that. You couldn't possibly. No blame attaches to you, none at all. I really don't want you to feel bad about it.'

I gulped my gratitude. The old gentleman seemed to get a grip on himself, motioned to me to sit down and took a seat himself opposite me, beside the blazing and comforting log fire. A reluctant bachelor myself, I envied him the cosy domesticity he had enjoyed for all these years.

'But I have to know,' he said with a weary sigh. 'I have to know, for my own peace of mind – I realize that sounds ridiculous, but I can't think how else to put it – I have to know what lies behind all this. The truth, I suppose – we have an ineradicable need to know the truth, however painful it may turn out to be.'

A reflective pause.

'It's odd, isn't it?' the old man resumed. 'It's you who should be doing all the asking, not me. That's why you tried to get in touch with Kathleen, so you could ask her questions. And now here am I questioning you.'

'Yes, it is ironic. The fact is, nobody still alive appears to know anything substantial about this relationship. Buchanan covered his tracks obsessively during his lifetime, and to good effect. And it seems as if your wife was equally successful.'

I feared for a moment that I had gone too far, but Mr Duffus seemed oblivious to my momentary want of tact.

'So the only real evidence', he mused, 'lies in this novel – *First Class Single to Nowhere*?'

'That's correct. But you haven't read it?'

'No. However, if you don't mind, I'd like you to tell me about it.'

I took a deep breath. I had been rather dreading this moment, and hoping it would fail to materialize. It did flash across my mind to duck out of it by suggesting he would do better to read the novel himself, but I decided immediately that this would be cowardly, and even bad faith. I had brought this on the old man, after all, even though unwittingly, and I owed it to him to be frank. I wanted him to trust me, too, to respect my directness, for I would need him on my side as I delved ever deeper in the course of my work. There was no saying what might turn up.

So I launched upon an analysis and interpretation of Buchanan's early masterpiece, realizing as I did so that what it conveys cannot be conveyed otherwise than as the author expressed it. At times I struggled. I concentrated, mainly, on the character – if that's the word for a presence who never makes a live appearance in the book – of Rosalind, which when all is said and done is beyond doubt the heart of the matter. It proved impossible to be evasive. I could not flinch from speaking of the depravity and infamy which Stoddart ends by attributing to Rosalind, even though their substance remains elusive and their reality at times appears ambiguous. I'm afraid that at some points in my narration I got rather carried away in my enthusiasm for the great novel, laying it on a bit thick about Rosalind and her turpitude and even forgetting for an instant that I was talking to the husband of the late original. But I did, recalling myself, urge Mr Duffus to keep always in mind that this was a work of fiction, and although undoubtedly grounded in solid autobiographical fact, still situated principally within the subjectivity of the protagonist.

When I finished and looked once more at the old man (I had not been much conscious of his presence while caught up in my flow), I was rather shocked to see that he looked grey and haggard and had visibly aged during the past few minutes.

'I suppose I shall have to read the damned book,' he muttered at length. 'Where can I get hold of it?'

I told him it was readily available but that I would be very happy to send him a copy as a token of my gratitude for his co-operation and understanding.

'I don't want my daughter to learn anything about this,' he said suddenly. 'I'd be grateful if you don't approach her.'

I readily agreed: it was unlikely that she would have been able to shed any light on these matters.

'You know,' the bereaved husband said thoughtfully after some moments of silence, 'I could never have found it in my heart to believe my wife capable of what this writer alleges, had it not been for that dreadful letter I received yesterday. Fiction I could have dismissed, and I'm sure I would have done so. But after the manner of my wife's death, then this evidence from some unknown source, which appears to corroborate the character Buchanan gives her . . . I'm so confused, Dr Halliday. It all seems so utterly incompatible with my knowledge of the woman I've loved and lived with for half a century. But I'm a realist, Dr Halliday. At the end of the day, I'm a realist.'

I nodded mutely. There was nothing I could say to ease his pain. Before I left, I asked Mr Duffus if he could show me a photograph of his wife in her youth. There was one in the sitting-room of the old couple on a bench in their garden, taken, he told me, on the occasion of their diamond wedding anniversary; but it didn't tell me much. The old man agreed to my request, if a trifle reluctantly, disappeared and came back a few minutes later with a formal graduation picture. It showed a fine-looking young woman with a direct gaze and a modest smile on her lips, looking not altogether comfortable in her unaccustomed academic garb. Certainly a girl it would have been easy to fall in love with; but at the same time I found it a little disappointing. I got no sense from it of the *femme fatale*, the captivating but deceitful breaker of hearts evoked in Buchanan's teasing paragraphs. But no doubt I was naive to expect anything of the sort. That kind of quality doesn't come out in a photograph, especially a posed and formal one. However, it did provide me with an image to keep in my mind while I pursued her trail, someone I could try to imagine as those who remembered her reminisced.

Unfortunately, though, there didn't prove to be many such people available. Only two, in fact. Mr Duffus gave me a couple of names of enduring friends who had known Kathleen since childhood and still lived locally, and a week or so after I met him I came up again and interviewed both on the same day. The first was useless: she was clearly in the early stages of dementia, had difficulty in understanding what I was driving at, and kept leaving the subject in hand to meander inconsequently through a maze of complete irrelevancies. The other, Mrs Ross, was altogether sharper. She was rather stiff and unaccommodating, though her memory, when she chose to exercise it, was good. She had kept in touch with her friend throughout her Edinburgh years, but she herself had been in Aberdeen for much of that time, and they had met only seldom. I asked her whether she knew what kind of circles Kathleen had moved in while in Edinburgh. She shrugged, I think sensing a leading question. Nothing out of the ordinary, so far as she knew. She certainly resisted strongly the suggestion that her friend had been in any way a 'bohemian'; indeed, I felt that she perhaps protested rather too much on this score. I asked her specifically whether she was aware of Kathleen's having known any writers. At first this drew no response; but then, a recollection seemingly coming to her, she said she did seem to recall a male friend – no more than that, certainly not a 'beau' – who had literary aspirations. She had no idea what had become of him, though.

'Was the name by any chance Buchanan?' I asked her, leaning forward eagerly as I felt the excitement of the chase mounting in me.

'Buchanan? . . . Yes, it might have been. That's possible.' She thought a little more, her old eyes searching the distance dreamily. 'Or was it Buchan? Yes, I rather think that it was Buchan.' Another pause. Then:

'Anyway, of course, I never met him.'

All of this was very frustrating. I had made what seemed like an exciting breakthrough when the minor literary figure had given me the name, but it had come too late. Not only had the possessor of that name died on me when the prize she represented – not so long before an apparently forlorn hope – was all but within my grasp, but I had come on the scene just at the moment when the events I had to uncover were fading from human memory, disappearing irreclaimably with the wits and the rapidly expiring lives of those who might have recalled them. I was reminded, not for the first time in my career as a recorder of others' lives, how tenuous and transient are the traces most of us leave on earth – we who think our lives so solid, real and substantial – and that this remained true even for those who, like Alexander Buchanan, had done something to make themselves remembered by more than friends and loved ones, and after those had themselves gone the way of all flesh.

But biographers are resilient creatures, and inclined to be hopeful. I knew from experience that in circumstances like these the only thing to do was to turn from the immediate problem to some more tractable aspect of the task in hand. There were plenty of loose ends to be tied up for Buchanan's later years, and sources were not hard to come by. I busied myself with these and left it to Fate to resolve the enigma of Rosalind, if she were so minded.

A couple of months passed.

Then one fine summer morning as I was sitting at my desk, just thinking that I would have to wrap my project up and send the book off to the publisher if nothing turned up soon on the Caldwell front, who should ring up but my old friend Nancy Cameron, who at that time had the Atholl Browse second-hand bookshop in Blair Atholl.

Nancy knew I was working on a biography of Buchanan – we had talked about it at some length on the occasion of my last visit – and, although she wasn't aware of these latest developments, was always on the lookout for anything which might have the slightest relevance to my project. She had found a reference to Buchanan in what she called a 'manuscript source' in amongst a consignment of books which a friend had cleared from the home of an old lady in Glasgow, who had recently moved into a nursing home. Nancy had found it intriguing and thought that I would too. There was a provoking sense of mystery about the whole thing which I enjoyed; so instead of pressing her for more details on the phone I arranged to take a trip up to Perthshire the very next day.

I always enjoyed visiting the Atholl Browse, with its endearing atmosphere of organized chaos and the promise of exciting discoveries in unlikely corners. Nancy poured me a cup of coffee, then drew from under a shelf beside the desk a slim volume which turned out to be a kind of yearbook on the theme of old Edinburgh. There was a print or drawing on each left-hand page, and facing it a page divided into four dates, so that the year was covered in about ninety pages. It was not a diary in the usual sense, in that days of the week were not named, so the book could be used in any year. Throughout the volume there were scattered entries, giving a random impression: sometimes there would be a concentration of entries for several days, then nothing for a few weeks, then an odd entry here and there, then another cluster. Each date had space for several brief entries, and for some there might be one for more than one year, while many others were left blank. The entries were written very neatly, in black ink, in a fine, resolute hand, and were absolutely uniform in character. Each consisted of a year, a man's name, and a place; mostly in Edinburgh, in which case there was usually a partial address or the name of a district in the city – but sometimes elsewhere, in which case only (say) 'Glasgow' or 'London' would appear. The earliest entries were for the year 1935 and the last for 1939. To give a few examples:

'George Hendry, Drumsheugh Gardens' occurred frequently during 1935 and the early part of 1936, then petered out. 'Jack Imrie, Glasgow' appeared occasionally in all the years. In 1938 and 1939 there were several fairly widely separated clusters featuring 'Julian Heath, London'. Another recurrent name was 'Archie MacDonald, Howe Street'. Quite a number of names, however, appeared only once or twice; and among them, directed by Nancy, I soon found the one I had quickly realized must be there somewhere. The date was 15 March, and the entry read, '1937. Alexander Buchanan, Marchmont.' In 1937 the future novelist had been in the last year of his honours history course at the university, and was living in lodgings in Marchmont Crescent.

It was inescapably clear to me that this could be nothing other than a woman's record of when and where she had slept with her assorted lovers. Buchanan's name appeared only once. I ascertained this before turning, with wild excitement and equal trepidation, to the title page, where I hoped the diarist might have written her own signature. I was not disappointed. There, inscribed neatly in the top right-hand corner in the same fine hand, was the name 'C. Caldwell'.

All the official documents I had seen had spelt 'Kathleen' with a K, but the name could of course equally be spelt with a C. I concluded that Miss Caldwell had preferred the latter (as indeed I did myself) and had adopted it, at least informally.

I now had virtually irrefutable proof that Buchanan had – almost certainly only once – had physical relations with the woman he fictionalized as 'Rosalind'. This resolved one of the great unanswered questions about the whole mysterious business; and the fact that it had been only once confirmed several of my hunches as to the nature of the relationship, and shed a great deal of light on the complex ambiguities of its treatment in the great but perplexing novel. Not to mention those repeated cryptic references to 'the Ides of March'! It was a good afternoon's work. I quickly agreed a price with Nancy for what to me was almost literally a priceless volume, and set off for home in a euphoric state.

It is only on the basis of this euphoria that I can excuse myself for what I did next. I was so excited that I felt compelled to phone Mr Duffus to tell him of this latest development. I think that at the back of my mind there was an inchoate feeling that he would want to know his wife had not, so to speak, died in vain: that the truth which her death had threatened to obscure had found an unexpected means of revealing itself. But it was an ill-judged decision. The old man sounded weary and dispirited even when he answered the phone.

'Oh, I see. You've discovered a list of my wife's lovers,' he said bleakly when I had told him of my discovery. And he made it clear that he did not wish to prolong the conversation. That was the last time I spoke to him.

It was about a fortnight after Mr Duffus's funeral, which I attended, that I met once again with the informant to whom I owed so much, but towards whom I felt oddly little gratitude. I had an increasing sense that he knew a good deal more than he had cared to let on, and was probably counting on being able to release his information in small doses to his own advantage. All I could do was squeeze him as best I could. When I saw the tired, cynical little face turn round to greet me from a bar stool in the Café Royal I felt so repelled that I had to struggle not to show it. Maybe I didn't succeed.

I started by thanking him for the help he had already given me, and began to open up about the discoveries to which this had led. To begin with, as I was getting into my stride, I'm afraid I misinterpreted the amused smirk on his self-satisfied features as admiration for the shrewdness and competence with which I had handled the investigation; but soon I noticed that he was looking down into his beer and passing his hand over his mouth with an affected air of trying to suppress laughter, a gesture which could only be seen as mocking. But when I came to the death of Mrs Duffus, he looked sharply up with an almost shocked expression, and the amused sneer, which he had as it were forgotten to erase, mingled rather horribly with something quite different, something indeed that resembled fear. He held up his hand to stop me.

'Hold on, Alan! There's something I have to tell you at this point. I was waiting for a suitable pause. I'm afraid you've got the name wrong.'

My stomach lurched sickeningly. I stared at him with my mouth open.

'Yes, I'm afraid so. The name was not Kathleen Caldwell, but Christine.'

'What? . . . You said Kathleen, I swear you did!' I could not imagine that if there had been the slightest indistinctness in his pronunciation I would have failed, in such a crucial matter, to have noticed it.

But he shook his head solemnly. 'No. Christine Caldwell. You've got the wrong person. This woman was not from Brechin, she was from Glasgow, and I don't think she was ever at the university. I believe she worked in an architect's office in some capacity.'

'But I thought you didn't know any more about her than what you told me last time?'

The wretched creature shrugged his shoulders. 'I don't know much more than that. It was just what I listened in to on that occasion . . . It was the name you wanted, and I gave it to you. Christine Caldwell.'

I remembered the ***C*** of the signature on the yearbook and knew that what he was now saying was true. I also realized he had previously lied to me deliberately, out of malice and to make a fool of me. He must somehow have known of the existence of this other Caldwell, Kathleen Caldwell, who had been around Edinburgh at the same time and with whom the other could be fatally confused. Clearly he knew a great deal more than he had let on, and what he did know was almost certainly invaluable. Equally clearly, though, it was out of the question to trust him further. Furious and humiliated, I excused myself without pretence of hiding my feelings and left him sitting at the bar.

As I made my way home through the busy summer streets my thoughts were in turmoil. After frustration and fury my first feeling was of relief – it could not, after all, have been shock at the contents of my letter which killed Mrs Duffus. If she were not the original of Rosalind, not the woman who had betrayed Buchanan, tortured him and lied to him, then even if she had known him – as old Mrs Ross's uncertain memory of a literary friend who could have been Buchanan, or Buchan, might possibly suggest – my inoffensive communication could scarcely have caused an access of emotion sufficient to have ended her life. Her death at that moment could have been nothing but coincidence.

But later I began to wonder. Coincidences do occur all the time in life – come to think of it, the fortuitous appearance of the precious yearbook amongst the consignment passed on to my friend Nancy could scarcely be anything else – but I have been a biographer long enough never to be quick to attribute to coincidence (leaving aside the fascinating but debatable phenomenon of synchronicity) what could have some other explanation. That Buchanan knew, around the same time, two young women with the surname Caldwell could, for instance, be accounted for by the possibility that they were related. He could, let us surmise, have met Kathleen first, at the university, and been introduced by her to her cousin Christine. And if Buchanan's feelings for Kathleen had never been more than those of friendship, what might have been hers towards him? Had one cousin loved Buchanan, and Buchanan loved the other? And had the heart of the honourable one broken as she saw the emotions of the man she loved taken captive and held in thrall by her morally worthless relative? If so, what might have been the onrush of feeling when all this was suddenly brought back to her, one ordinary morning of her serene old age?

Yes, it was all now falling quite neatly into place.

But isn't there a loose end? you may be thinking. Something that doesn't fit in at all with this theory – that appears, indeed, flatly to contradict it? What about the 'letter of sympathy' to Mr Duffus, that infamous epistle which implied that his deceased wife had been precisely the sort of person characterized by Buchanan in his novel as the captivating, promiscuous and deceitful Rosalind? What are we to make of that?

Well, dear friends, I have a confession to make – ***I*** wrote that letter. I am not proud of it. But in my trade one sometimes has to resort to tricks which one would, in an ideal world, prefer to shun, just to induce people who might otherwise be reticent or unco-operative to talk spontaneously. A sudden shock like the one I had hoped to produce with that letter – it does often work. In this case, of course, it didn't, for reasons that are clear enough. But I had no way of knowing that at the time.

Anyway, in my occupation one is always having to make fresh starts, and all the time I spent on tracking down Kathleen Caldwell will not, I'm sure, turn out to have been wasted. I'm very much back in business now, and raring to go, thanks to that serendipitous discovery among the books of old Mrs Imrie.

But I have a suspicion that Christine Caldwell will prove a hard nut to crack.

2

The Blazing Curate

The shocking and scandalous events I have to tell you about took place in a county in Scotland which shall remain nameless, for reasons which will become apparent. Or rather, not strictly in a county, because counties now exist only on paper, and paper in a particular form what is more, namely that of an envelope, for you're allowed to use the name of a former county as part of a postal address but, so far as I'm aware, in no other way. So, the events took place in a region; though not in a strict administrative sense, for regions in that sense no longer exist, in spite of the fact that many official bodies still use the names of former regions as part of their titles, illicitly I would venture to suggest.

It might be safer, then, to say that these events took place in a constituency. Indeed, it may be true to say that they took place in two constituencies, a 'Westminster' constituency and a 'Holyrood' constituency; though in another sense these two constituencies were only one constituency, since they shared the same name and had identical boundaries. But to address that extremely interesting question satisfactorily it would be necessary to invoke, and to examine with some thoroughness, Leibniz's Principle of the Identity of Indiscernibles, and tempting though that prospect is, I think we must reluctantly conclude that this is neither the time nor the place. Anyway, this constituency, or these constituencies, will remain nameless, because of the anguish their identification would cause to the two sitting Members representing them in the 'Westminster' and 'Holyrood' parliaments respectively, both men (they are, I'm afraid, both men) I admire, though not without reservations; to them, and to others too.

The scandalous events in question took place in a small Scottish Episcopal church in a village in that constituency which, with equally good reason and for very similar reasons, will also remain nameless. They arose when a young man got up in the pulpit one Easter Sunday morning and stated, in the course of his sermon, that Jesus raised himself from the dead. This young man was known locally as 'the curate', though so far as I'm aware there are no curates in Scotland, any more than there are squires, and never have been – but I could be wrong about that. Probably he was called the curate because there were so many English incomers in the village in question, and English incomers are accustomed to curates.

But what are curates, after all? They are insipid young men after whom young ladies languish in the novels of Jane Austen, are they not? And this young man, though certainly insipid, would never have been admitted into a novel by Jane Austen. He had a bead in his nose, for one thing, and curates in novels by Jane Austen never have beads in their noses. It simply wasn't the fashion in those days. At any rate, I prefer to think of this young man as some kind of probationer, though I'm aware that this term is not technically correct. For all I know he may have been a deacon; though whether a deacon would normally be allowed to preach a sermon on Easter Sunday I can't say. By the end of the service, at any rate, there were a great many people who wished he hadn't.

Now to say that Jesus raised himself from the dead, though in terms of orthodox Christian theology a lamentable *faux pas* to say the least,[1] would normally nowadays raise scarcely an eyebrow in most churches, I think I can assert. Because these days it's generally accepted that it's up to individuals to make up their own minds about these things, the days of being instructed how to think from a pulpit by some patriarchal figure in a dog-collar are deemed to be long gone. And the curate's, or deacon's, or probationer's odd remark might in itself have given rise to no scandal at all, had not Walkinshaw risen to his feet to challenge it. There are some who would have it that Walkinshaw did so only because he was off his head, but I think myself that that's an unduly harsh

---

[1] In point of fact this is questionable. It might plausibly be argued that the curate's remark was completely orthodox: that, while to say that Jesus raised himself from the dead was indeed to make an unaccustomed and daring emphasis, the fact remains that, since Jesus was fully God as well as fully Man, the statement was dogmatically unexceptionable.

But let that pass.

way to put it. Someone, groping for an appropriate way of expressing it, suggested that he had learning difficulties, but really that is quite wide of the mark, because in reality Walkinshaw was a more than competent learner, even something of a scholar by the standards of the local community. My own view is that he suffered from a personality disorder; but alas, there are still some who insist on repeating the fiction that he was off his head.

Why Walkinshaw felt called upon to make this stand is altogether unclear. He didn't, it seems, have any immovable conviction himself about what, if anything, took place at the Resurrection. In some sense, perhaps, he believed in it; but whether he believed in it literally, or symbolically, or in some mythological or esoteric sense, or in terms of personal transformation or what-not, or actually not at all in any sense: of all this he was quite unsure, I believe. Nonetheless, when the curate or whatever he was got up in the pulpit and stated, quite blatantly and without qualification – in a calculatedly provocative manner, it seemed, though in reality it may have been a matter simply of woolly subjectivity, or poor theological training, or even mere ignorance and stupidity – that Jesus raised himself from the dead, Walkinshaw saw red.

Why, exactly?

Well, because, as I understand it, Walkinshaw had always been given to believe that the correct theological position was that Jesus was raised from the dead by God the Father, and that in past ages people had been burned at the stake for doctrinal solecisms far less heinous than the one he had just heard. And all this that Walkinshaw had been given to believe was, I dare say, perfectly correct: in terms, that is, of orthodox Christian theology. Moreover,

Walkinshaw felt that whatever doubts, uncertainties, or difficulties in understanding he might personally experience in relation to the doctrine of the Resurrection, what he expected from the pulpit on an Easter Sunday morning was orthodox Christian theology. Especially since what the curate had pronounced was not, or did not appear to be, delivered in any spirit of creatively reinterpreting doctrine, understanding these events differently in the light of current scientific knowledge, or anything of that kind however nebulous, but was simply asserted blandly, and at the same time also wrong.

That is about as much as I can offer (while bearing in mind my suspicion that Walkinshaw was the victim of a personality disorder) to elucidate what followed after the curate, or whatever he was, stated that Jesus raised himself from the dead.

Walkinshaw stood up without ceremony or hesitation. Or if there was any hesitation, it cannot have been of significant duration. He had to grab the moment, after all, and the curate's pause could not be expected to last long. His action was impulsive, no doubt, but at the same time it was convinced; and he spoke in a firm, clear voice.

'That is theological drivel,' he said.

It could have been put more kindly, I dare say, but for someone with a personality disorder putting things kindly does not always come easily. At least he left no room for doubt.

The curate blushed and smiled weakly, as curates do. Or so I have always imagined. Then he laughed, also weakly, and scratched an ear lobe. He should certainly not have laughed. It was no laughing matter, viewed from any angle.

No-one else laughed, that much is certain. Quite a number gasped, or turned round and looked at Walkinshaw, or stirred uneasily in their seats. Some looked not at Walkinshaw but at the curate, to gauge his reaction. Others kept very still and looked modestly and steadfastly at their knees, as if anything else they might venture could only make matters worse. Several people, it seems, shook their heads. But a shake of the head can mean so many things. It could have indicated on this occasion, for instance, horror at the curate's heresy, or contrariwise, dissent from Walkinshaw's objection, or perhaps shocked disapproval of the impropriety of his intervention, irrespective of the undoubted correctness of its content. Did anyone, on the other hand, nod? It has been suggested to me that at least one person did, a very respectable and intelligent elderly gentleman, a former county archivist. If he indeed did so, it is almost certain that it was in agreement with Walkinshaw, and it may be that Walkinshaw was aware of this and that it encouraged him to intensify his protest. The Rector meanwhile, who was actually conducting the service although the probationary chap was preaching, felt called upon to assert his priestly authority and pour oil on these very troubled waters.

'Why don't we agree to thrash it out later?' he suggested mildly, advancing from the sanctuary and smiling vaguely, while looking around the congregation as if to invite a consensus. 'This doesn't seem to be the time . . . '

No-one said anything; Walkinshaw had resumed his seat, breathing heavily, and the curate appeared to conclude from all this, quite mistakenly as it transpired, that the appealed-for agreement had been reached. He cleared his throat, smiled weakly once more, and made to resume his sermon where he had left off, for all the world as if nothing at all had happened – or at most as if there had been some very unimportant hiatus, such as might have occurred for instance if he had lost his place or had a slight coughing fit.

'What all this goes to show . . . ' he began, in quite a strong voice, though it may have held the ghost of a tremor . . .

And then – and then!

'Burn him at the stake!' shouted Walkinshaw, without rising from his seat but stabbing the air with his finger. 'Burn him at the stake!'

The silence following this proposal was probably as close to absolute as can be imagined. The retired county archivist's head was seen to rise and fall in what, in almost any other circumstances, could only have been interpreted as a nod; but it is surely inconceivable that on this occasion it can really have signified assent!

But perhaps the curate observed it and so understood it. At any rate he stopped talking and blanched, as if he had eaten a not very fresh egg for breakfast. His mouth hung open a little and his eyes flickered wildly around the congregation. Then he simply turned and fled. The little door of the pulpit refused at first to open to his fumbling fingers. When he did get out he almost threw himself down the three steps from the altar, with the result that he at once lost his balance, and throwing out his arms overturned the lighted paschal-candle and pitched on top of it. Almost instantly his voluminous alb, saturated with years of accumulated chrism oil and candle grease, burst into flames. The curate wallowed on the ground, howling, then began crawling down the aisle. Everybody had stood up and naturally pandemonium ensued, with people emitting exclamations of horror, shouting suggestions as to how to deal with this unprecedented situation, and in some cases already shoving and elbowing in their efforts to get out of the threatened church. To make matters worse there were far more people in the rather small building than usual, this being Easter Sunday, and in fact probably considerably more than fire regulations would have permitted. They were in their best clothes, too, and anxious that these should not be singed. The Rector, perhaps feeling that the moment was beyond him, or maybe simply getting his priorities right, was busily intent on setting the paschal-candle to rights. He even found a box of matches in a pocket of his cassock and set about re-lighting the candle, while the curate writhed and moaned on the carpet.

And now, above all the hubbub, rang out the crazed voice of Walkinshaw:

'The judgement of God!' he cried repeatedly. 'The judgement of *God!*'

As to the retired archivist, he could be heard remarking *sotto voce* to Walkinshaw:

'By all means let us have nonsense in church, but at least let it be coherent nonsense.'

An extraordinary degree of confusion now prevailed. The curate, perhaps in his panic not realizing what exactly had caused the conflagration, may himself have believed that he was the victim of God's judgement for his blasphemy, or alternatively may have supposed that his offended audience had taken Walkinshaw's proposal to heart and had deliberately set him alight. He was howling for mercy at any rate, whether from God or man. The congregation, meanwhile, were deeply divided. Some, either from Christian charity or from fear that the conflagration must ultimately engulf the church and destroy both the building and everyone in it, were seeking means of dousing the blazing curate, which was not a straightforward task as the church had no water supply. A small but select body, on the other hand, appeared to be of Walkinshaw's opinion and felt that, since God had apparently intervened in so decisive and unequivocal a fashion and moreover with such competence and celerity, things must be allowed to take their inevitable course: any attempt to save the curate might indeed in such circumstances make them conspirators after the event. A third group, and that the largest, and consisting mainly of the non-regular attenders, were intent merely on saving their own skins; they were trying to get out of the church as fast as they could and at the same time to keep as far away as possible from the burning heretic.

But crises of any kind almost always throw up a hero, or, as in this case, a heroine – in the shape of a large lady in late middle age, an exemplary pillar of the church, who now grabbed hold unhesitatingly of a beautiful flower arrangement in a large vase, the work in fact of her own hands, and emptied it, flowers and water, unceremoniously but with unerring aim over the most flaming part of the curate's alb, and succeeded thus in extinguishing the most threatening of the flames.

My own feeling is that the extent of the blaze must have been somewhat exaggerated by the rather hysterical people who reported all this to me. The curate, it is true, had lost consciousness at this point, but I think more from fright than from severe injury. He was still smouldering in places, though; and when Walkinshaw, who seems to have become something of a figure of authority in the course of this crisis (the rector, having successfully re-lit the paschal-candle, had retreated to the sanctuary and appeared to be rapt in prayer) – when Walkinshaw cried out, 'Dunk him in the burn!' there were plenty of willing hands to carry out his orders. Now that any immediate danger to their own persons appeared to have been averted, everyone was anxious to show willing and participate in these stirring events. Half a dozen good men and true stepped forward and like pall-bearers lifted the senseless probationer aloft. Then, the crowd parting before them, they ran down the aisle at a kind of military trot, and out of the church door, towards the substantial burn which ran by the side of the graveyard at about fifty yards' distance, in its delightful rustic setting. In the enthusiasm of the moment forgetting all about their Easter best, they gamely waded into the burn and, making use of a good-sized pool, immersed and then withdrew the smouldering cleric.

As he emerged from the waters the curate briefly regained consciousness and whispered, 'Tell Laura I love her,' before lapsing once more into oblivion. Laura was as it happens the name of the curate's wife, and it is unlikely that he intended any reference to the nauseating pop song of 1960 which bears a title identical to these words, and tells of the dying message to the girl he loves of a young man fatally injured in a stock-car race. However that may be, this context renders his remark deeply ironic. For the stalwart who had hold of the curate's shoulder, in leaning towards the young man's ear in an effort to catch his meaning, unluckily lost his footing on the slippery bed of the burn, toppled over and loosed his grip on the greasy alb. The commotion of his fall caused all the rest of the bearers either to lose their own grip or unthinkingly to let go as they tried to grab hold of their companion, a well-known and popular figure in the village.

Before anyone knew it, the curate was floating free. In normal circumstances this would scarcely have mattered, but that day, by ill chance, the stream was in full spate following two consecutive days of heavy rain, and flowing with unusual dispatch. By the time the fallen pall-bearer had been rescued and the others began to think once more about the hapless curate, he was far downstream, floating rapidly on his back in his magnificent Easter alb towards the confluence of the Allt na Beinne with the Allt na Choire. Everyone – the entire congregation had by this time gathered by the side of the burn – rushed in their Easter finery down the parallel track, shouting and waving their arms as if this might make the curate reconsider his decision. One or two fast runners headed off across the fields in the hope of reaching the confluence before the curate did, but in vain. For quite a time he could still be seen, disappearing momentarily beneath the waves then resurfacing, the snowy whiteness of the alb caught by the beams of the lovely early spring sun. Thus he was borne on, like the Lady of Shalott floating down to Camelot or garland-draped Ophelia on her spread-out clothes, on to the fatal confluence and thence far, far away, out of history and into legend itself.

For the curate in his Easter alb has never been seen since; though it is said by some that he can be descried from time to time in the little church in the uncertain light of a winter's Sunday morning, hovering in the air just above the shoulder of some visiting preacher in danger of plunging unheedingly into turbulent theological waters, wagging an admonitory finger. And every Easter morning the rafters ring as Walkinshaw, in a very acceptable light baritone, leads the little congregation in the commemorative hymn composed by himself to mark their collective delivery from gross error:

(To the tune of
'The head that once was crowned with thorns')

O wretched curate, who didst say –
And that on Easter Day –
That Jesus Christ did raise himself
And bear himself away!

The Lord upspoke with tongue of fire
And flames of dreadful ire;
Till waters rose like Noah's flood
And dous'd that funeral pyre.

The Curate's Burn then burst its banks
And carried him away;
And may all wretches perish thus
Who lead their flocks astray.

3

The Owl of Soilluc

Malcolm Cormack was thrawnly determined to climb to the viewpoint on the top floor of the corner tower – the Tour du Moulin – of the fortifications of Soilluc. To stand up there and survey, once more, the glories of the medieval town and the surrounding valley. He had quarrelled violently with his wife about this certainly unnecessary detour on their way back from Provence, and she had gone on home without him. She had not, Cormack was convinced, understood anything at all of what he felt. But probably he had not explained it very well: for the truth was that he couldn't really explain it to himself.

He had last been in this part of France forty years before, when he was eighteen. Of all the memories of that time, the view from the Tour du Moulin stood out with the most pellucid clarity and still carried with it the fragrant aura of the hopes and longings of youth. He didn't deceive himself, of course, about how much he had lost since those far-off days – how few of those hopes had come to fruition. But perhaps precisely because of this sober recognition, he yearned the more painfully to recapture the feeling which had inspired him then. That feeling had had its own truth, however much it had since been eroded by time and life's realities. He could recapture that essence still – could he not? – feel it again as he had felt it then, if only he could stand once more on the topmost tower of the fortifications of Soilluc. So at least he told himself.

When his wife had dropped him at the station he had been desperate to get rid of her, to be by himself; but – in one of those discomfiting reversals of feeling to which he remained distressingly prone – once he found himself alone in his hotel room at Soilluc he was suddenly and quite unexpectedly overwhelmed with loneliness and desolation. More than that: with dread.

The next morning, though, when he set out after breakfast to rediscover the town, his mind had papered over this gaping crack. The weather was fine without being too hot, a refreshing breeze was blowing which he found liberating after the sometimes oppressive air of the south. His back was beginning to recover its suppleness after the previous day's long drive. Especially after he had succeeded in crossing the bridge from the island on which his hotel was situated, Cormack felt more like his old self, the remote self of his youth. For some years now he had increasingly been afflicted with vertigo. As soon as he had noticed, from the window of the hotel restaurant, how low the parapet was, and how much traffic was constantly rushing to and fro over the bridge, he had begun to be nervous about making this crossing.

And indeed it had not proved a pleasant experience. The pavement was ridiculously, yes irresponsibly narrow. He had either to stick close to the crazily low parapet and remain constantly aware – though he couldn't look at it directly – of the sickeningly deep drop to the swift, pale-brown waters of the broad river below, or else risk stumbling (especially if he had to pass or overtake another pedestrian) into the rush of the oncoming traffic, which dashed past frenetically and without ceasing, pitilessly indifferent to his plight. As often when he was frightened, his feeling shifted imperceptibly into rage, rage at this mindless onrush of the traffic and at the vain purposefulness of the drivers – empty, as he conceived it, of value and meaning; and this rage sustained him and drove him on, and got him at last safely to the other side of the bridge.

Soilluc was as he remembered it, so far as outward appearance was concerned. There had been some redevelopment, no doubt, during the intervening forty years, and a new road swept through an underpass to a huge new car park close to the fortifications; but the core of the old town remained unspoilt and full of liveliness and atmosphere, and Cormack wandered around the medieval streets with a vague sense of self-satisfaction. He could so easily, after all, have lived out the remainder of his life without ever having seen Soilluc again. He had always refused to go along with the received wisdom that one should never return to the places one has loved in youth. Cormack was on the contrary a great returner, partly perhaps because of a certain timidity in his nature which made him seek out the familiar and shy away from new experience; and he felt obscurely that he had to justify that tendency by getting the most out of his nostalgic revisiting.

At first it seemed to be working. Soilluc was still

beautiful; and, yes, he could see that it was so. Nothing seemed, at first, to be wrong. It was only after the visit to the cathedral that he became aware of a certain unease, a curious failure of satisfaction. Was it because of the irritation he felt at having constantly to put his glasses on and take them off again? Partly, no doubt. That was certainly an impediment to the freshness and spontaneity of one's responses. Was that why he seemed to be succeeding so little, as he now realized, in feeling what he felt he ought to be feeling? But it could scarcely be only that. As he gazed at the splendour of the Romanesque arches, at the delicate intricacy of the wood carvings, at the richness and miraculous artistry of the tapestries, the truth of his own inner emptiness was vaguely but insistently borne in upon him, and cast a heavy pall of gloom over his spirit.

He had made up his mind to leave the fortifications until the last, like a child saving the best bit of the pudding until the end; and he would complete the ritual with the Tour du Moulin. When he found himself on the battlements a real sense of excitement rose in him at last, as he approached the old tower with its solid stone gateway over which was carved with pleasing naivety the town's ancient emblem: the famous owl which, according to legend, was wont to appear in order to warn the inhabitants of impending disaster from plague, fire, famine or sword. Or, rather than warn, did its appearance rather *presage* these events, as some had always held? The tradition was equivocal, the figure of the owl ambiguous and sinister. The Owl of Soilluc had been feared as much as honoured, placated more than loved.

Cormack raised his hand, intending to give the owl's

beak an affectionate tweak, but the bird stared back at him coldly and forbiddingly, and he dropped his hand again with a superstitious grue. Looking quickly away, he raced up the stairs to the first level and, ignoring its four broad windows with their magnificent views of the town and surrounding countryside, turned eagerly to the steps ascending to the topmost floor of the tower; and was met by a metal grille on which was appended a large sign in black and red lettering:

ENTREE INTERDITE AU PUBLIC
DANGER DE MORT

Cormack gasped aloud with frustration and annoyance. A part of him simply refused to accept what he read. What nonsense was this? What danger? How was this view more dangerous than it had ever been? Why were they doing this to him? There had been no *Danger de Mort* forty years ago!

It was this cursed modern obsession with safety that was to blame: a crazy obsession, an over-valuation of life which surely sprang from a fear of death, an unacknowledged fear which nowadays lay deeply hidden and obscured at the back of every mind which no longer believed in an afterlife. Hence this idiocy which was depriving him of the satisfaction which he craved and to which he had looked forward with what he obscurely realized was quite exaggerated expectation. The idiocy which now debarred him from the perspective from which he had once surveyed the world and his future with such zestful aspiration.

He turned away, baffled and defeated. But the odd thing

was that there was also in his reaction an element of relief. For in truth he had been pressing away, ever since he had formed the idea of this visit, a fear that he would experience disabling vertigo on the highest level of the fortifications. The affliction had never troubled him in his youth; it had been an insidious and relatively recent development. He was deeply ashamed of this weakness, and resented its hold over him. Perhaps it was partly to prove to himself that he was not its slave that he had formed the resolve to climb once more to the summit of the Tour du Moulin. So the measure of relief which was taking the edge off his resentment now seemed to him the more shameful, the mark of a pitiful falling-away in his general relation to life.

Cormack wandered over to the opposite side of the courtyard and descended once more, almost absent-mindedly, into the subterranean dungeon which he had looked into some time earlier. There was a warm darkness down there, and in the gloom he could make out a large, shallow puddle which had formed in a declivity and which was perhaps a more or less permanent feature of these murky depths. It was in just such filthy holes that incarcerated heroines of Gothic novels had languished for weeks and months, lost to the world and to time, in unrelieved, impenetrable darkness and bone-chilling damp, prey to the attentions of loathsome and lascivious reptiles which crawled over their bodies during their uneasy sleep and fastened themselves lovingly on their breasts. Cormack remained down there for some minutes, musing upon all of this, finding an odd pleasure and excitement in these distasteful images.

It was now well on in the afternoon and he began to

wander, by a roundabout route, back in the direction of his hotel. A deathly depression had settled upon his heart. Seeing a church which he had not visited before, for it was not lauded in any of the tourist guides, he stepped in to kill a little time. An organ was tootling away desultorily and two young girls were standing talking and laughing near the top of the nave, music sheets in their hands. It was a Saturday afternoon and they were evidently taking a short break during a rehearsal for tomorrow's High Mass. Cormack didn't really feel like listening to this rehearsal, expecting to hear the saccharine notes of some sentimental contemporary religious music. He was turning to go when the organ started up, and after a few notes he realized that they were rehearsing the Gloria from Mozart's C Minor Mass.

The girls' voices rose in what was for him at that moment an unimaginably beautiful and unlooked-for concert of praise and adoration. Soprano and mezzo-soprano, they answered each other, met and parted and came together again in an incomparable pattern of sacred sound which for a few moments invoked and reanimated his crumbling and decaying faith.

Laudamus te,
benedicimus te,
adoramus te,
glorificamus te . . .

Tears came to his eyes, watering his parched spirit, giving Cormack a fleeting hope that flesh might grow once more upon the dry bones of his life.

Yet at the same time he felt himself debarred from that

hope by the reality of his faithlessness. The Gloria came to an end and he went quickly out, wanting to keep the memory of the music whole in his mind as he walked back to the hotel. In the hot glare of the sun a down-and-out, doubly amputated below the knees, was moving with odd swiftness along the pavement on his hands and rump. As they passed and Cormack stared with pity and horror, the man gave him a hard, contemptuous look which in his feverish state of mind he suddenly associated with the carving of the owl.

Cormack shuddered and walked on.

In the hotel restaurant that evening he sat alone, feeling old, discontented and unsettled. The freshness and excitement of the moment of his arrival at Soilluc had faded into the past, and soon it would seem as dim and distant as his first arrival forty years before. Now a perverse idea, born of his sense of failure and resentment, had lodged itself at the back of his mind: that tomorrow he would defy the prohibition at the tower and climb to the top.

The bottle of local wine fuelled his defiance and formed a protective film over his depression, and he began to relish his rabbit fricassee. Some monoglot tourists from Lancashire at a nearby table were having difficulty in communicating their desire for a jug of water to the waitress. Cormack was able to help out and felt childishly pleased with himself. Then immediately he experienced a desire to distance himself from these tourists, and to demonstrate to the waitress that not everyone from across the Channel was so crass and ignorant, and that the Scots in particular came into a quite different category. He decided rashly that he would show off his French when the waitress came to take away his plate.

'*En Ecosse*', he began confidently, '*c'est difficile d'obtenir le lapin, à cause de la myxomatose . . . la maladie aux lapins?*' he continued uncertainly, and with mounting anxiety when the girl seemed not to understand. '*Les yeux*,' he stammered, searching unsuccessfully in his mind for the word for 'swollen', '*aveugles . . .* '

'*Ah, oui!*' The waitress appeared shocked, and Cormack suddenly realized with surging embarrassment that what he had said might be taken to imply that the French were careless about the possible effects of eating rabbits afflicted with myxomatosis! That had not been his intention at all. To make matters worse, he was also not at all sure how idiomatic or even correct his French had been; it had not rolled off his tongue with the confidence promised when he had rehearsed the sentences in his mind. He came to the conclusion that he had undoubtedly made a complete fool of himself, and once again felt ashamed and obscurely resentful.

In bed that night the rabbit fricassee lay heavily on his stomach. The smallish bedroom was rather stuffy and sleep failed to come. As he tossed and turned it began to occur to him that it was perhaps really not all that safe to eat rabbit. Suppose it *had* been infected? 'Myxomatosis leaps the species barrier!' – he seemed to read the newspaper headline. His eyes felt dry and itchy. He got up, turned on the light and looked in the mirror. And yes, his eyelids certainly seemed a bit puffy. He got back into bed but still failed to sleep. At about one o' clock someone came noisily into the room next door and began banging doors and slamming drawers shut without any thought for his neighbours. Gripped by fury, Cormack got up, thumped on the wall and shouted sarcastically:

'*Un peu plus de bruit, s'il vous plaît!*'

But there was no response.

As he got back into bed, Cormack saw clearly enough in the moonlight that streamed into the bedroom a great owl swoop down and alight on the rail of the balcony. It seemed to gaze intently in at him for a moment, tilting its head a little, and in that instant he had a sense of a powerful, wordless communication, as if there was no barrier between the bird and him and they were speaking soul to soul, though he was unable to grasp the content of what was said. The impression came and went so swiftly that it might almost have been illusory; then the owl opened its wings once more and disappeared into the night. Cormack sank back on his pillow and was almost instantly asleep.

Some time later, Cormack dreamt he was eating a very rich and indigestible meal in the great banqueting hall of the castle. He sat all by himself at a long candle-lit table, in the midst of dark, oppressive splendour. As he ate, he came slowly and with horror to understand that he was devouring the famous Owl of Soilluc. This was a fearful thing to do, he knew, and he began to weep as he ate. The tears he wept seemed to be corrosive, and when they fell on to the white table-cloth they hissed like acid and burned holes in the linen, which turned blue around the edges. He wanted to stop eating, but to do so would be to admit his terrible mistake, and this he couldn't bring himself to do. Then it seemed to be morning, and he was listening to a report on the radio.

'The Owl of Soilluc,' the announcer said gravely, 'one

of the rarest birds in Europe, is missing. Early today it was discovered to be absent from its usual domicile, and it has not been seen since.'

When he awoke in the morning, Cormack felt as if drugged. He knew that something fearful and unaccountable had happened to him during the night, but he couldn't get a hold on what it was. He was dazed, ill and disorientated, but one obsessive idea now dominated his thoughts: that yesterday he had accepted defeat too readily. There was only one way he could salvage his self-respect. After taking breakfast in his room he made his way, sick though he was, stubbornly once more across the bridge – aware, this time, only as in a confused dream, of the tormented traffic – and sought out the fortifications of Soilluc and the Tour du Moulin . . .

The barrier was of a makeshift nature and, it is clear, altogether too easy to negotiate. It is always easy to be wise after the event, of course, but everyone agreed that more effective measures would now be necessary.

4

Death and Devolution

Back in those heady days following Winnie Ewing's victory at the Hamilton by-election in 1967 – dim old days they seem now – several of us who called ourselves 'activists' in our obscure little SNP branch in Edinburgh were quite obsessed with the heroic days of Irish nationalism, and particularly with the events surrounding the Easter Rising. Our heroes were Connolly and Pearse, and MacDonagh and MacDermott and McBride, and especially, perhaps, the 'noble Cathal Brugha', who, we were quite disconcerted to discover eventually, was in fact an Englishman. We used to read aloud Yeats's 'Easter 1916' and secretly, shyly, in our hearts imagined some future Scottish poet eulogizing ourselves in like manner. Nothing remotely like the Easter Rising was even distantly to be discerned on the Scottish horizon, of course – the stealing of the Stone years back and a few paltry explosions in pillar boxes was the most our heroic movement had to show in the way of 'direct action' – but Hugh MacDiarmid was blasting away as provocatively as ever, Wendy Wood was making symbolic gestures, and the 1320 Club was hinting darkly that the ballot box was going to fail us. Anything seemed possible at that time, and we were young.

There was a hard core of us in our branch who used to meet several times a week to address envelopes and go leafleting and see to the myriad other routine tasks which fall to the lot of tireless activists. Some of us, perhaps, were more tireless than others. There were Tommy and Alice, first of all, who were married and in whose house we met, and myself – we three did everything together. Then there were Dick Brown, a teacher like me, who was obsessed with westerns and used to carry a toy gun about with him, and a deeply earnest young man called Colin who was training for the ministry and who would infallibly defect to Labour when the moment was ripe. There was the slightly effeminate Jack Weir, and Cameron the ex-Liberal, who kept screwing his eyes up and pushing his glasses up on his nose. Then there was big Donald Lumb, who wore a flat kep and a belted raincoat and went shopping with his mother on a Saturday morning, and his equally big sidekick, Stutterin' Willie. So most of us were men and – with the exception, strangely enough, of Jack Weir, and of course Tommy and Alice – all single, and what used to be called 'sex-starved', a phrase which has largely vanished with the phenomenon to which it referred. Members, in fact, of 'the great unshagged', as someone once nicely put it.

So it was a red-letter day from more than one perspective when Tommy received a letter one fine morning from a prospective new branch member – an Irish girl who was studying at the Art College. I'll call her Niamh, because Irish girls are often called Niamh, though that was not her real name. And the repressed excitement was palpable on the mild summer evening when we awaited her arrival for the first working session which she had agreed, over the phone, to attend. Most of the others were hanging back nervously, but I confess that I was standing at the big window of Tommy and Alice's front room in Stockbridge when Niamh came down the street with long easy strides in her short summer skirt.

I had one overwhelming impression when I first saw Niamh, walking down the street that evening so long ago – that there was someone else walking invisibly beside her. I can't say in what it consisted or how it made itself known, or what it may have meant, nor can I explain it more exactly or in a different way; but it was an indelible inner impression which has never left me.

When she walked into that room which was full of ill-assorted people whom she had never met before, Niamh's composure was utterly undisturbed. It wasn't her beauty which caught at the heart, though she was beautiful in a quite traditional Irish way, with unreadable deep blue eyes and long dark hair and a slightly tip-tilted nose; it was her immediacy, in both a temporal and a spatial sense. She was with us, and at once. And naturally all the lang dreeps and muckle sumphs in the room who were still unmarried promptly fell in love with Niamh and fell over themselves to go leafleting with her, myself not excluded; though in justice to myself I have to add that I was the only one who ever stood a chance.

It was only after she had been around for a few weeks that Niamh let it slip that her grandfather had been in arms during the Easter Rising. Whether he had actually seen combat was not altogether clear, but he had worn the green, no doubt of that, and had been in sight of more than one of our deathless heroes. That was enough for us. Niamh was exalted in our eyes into one who had a part in a legend, and yet there she was among us, real and vibrant and alive, and perhaps even available.

Not that she let that be known. She became one of the gang, right enough, but sexually she was quite aloof, or so it seemed. We used to drink quite a lot in the hotels which were springing up about that time in the crescents around the fringes of the New Town – most of them have since reverted to domestic use. There we used to listen to second-rate folk groups who endeavoured to imitate the Corries and, though with little real hope, dreamed of emulating their success. And we used to go to folk events and ceilidhs all over town. Niamh, just because she was Irish and because her grandfather had worn the green in 1916, seemed to move among us, as we tirelessly and naively mulled over the impossible future in a dozen smoky bars, as a living pledge that this was not all just a romantic dream, that Scotland could do what Ireland had done, and that some time before we all died we would be living in a free Scotland, true sister to the nation of which Niamh was a proud citizen.

Gradually I began to feel that Niamh was moving towards me. I was so shy with women at that time as to be almost dysfunctional, so any running had to be made by her. I wasn't shy of her as a friend, it's true . . . but anything beyond that was a different matter. I was completely besotted with her, and had been almost from the start. So, among others, was big Donald Lumb. Donald had a genius for malapropisms and getting things upside down. Once Tommy warned him against getting too keen on Niamh and told him that if he tried anything on she would 'chew him up and spit him out'. 'Don't worry,' Donald reassured him. 'I've got my head planted firmly in the ground.' And one evening we were all talking about Cameron the ex-Liberal, who wasn't there. Tommy and I had been tearing him to pieces and Niamh had been pretending, out of contrariness, to take his part. Donald, naturally, rushed to agree with her.

'I like Bill, myself,' he announced. 'He's such a modest, self-defecating young guy.'

Niamh and I exchanged a look at that point, and it was that look, no doubt about it, which marked the turning-point in our relations. After that I began seeing her on her own sometimes, taking her to dances and ceilidhs and having a drink with her without the others, nothing more than that as yet. There was no doubt that she liked me, but there was something holding her back. Then one time when we were with Tommy and Alice she mentioned that there was a ceilidh-dance coming up at the University Nationalist Club, and would we like to go? She looked at the others questioningly first, I remember, then at me.

Yes, we would go, that was decided.

We were together, the four of us, that evening, and it was a good one. Then, after about an hour, an older man came into the hall. I saw him exchanging a look of recognition with Niamh; no, more than that, it was something more intimate than recognition. He stood by himself by the bar for some time with a beer in his hand while a singer was performing, a look of amused observation on his face, scanning the crowd, a look not quite of disdain but certainly of distance.

'That's Douglas Heron,' said Tommy. 'He used to be

around on the nationalist scene years ago, when I was just a lad.'

Niamh nodded and, I noticed, dropped her head a little. When the song finished Heron walked across to our table and asked politely if he could join us. Niamh introduced us and Tommy indicated that he already knew Heron, but Heron remained inscrutable. I saw at once that there was a tormented connection between him and Niamh. Soon he took her away to dance and for the rest of that evening I saw little of Niamh. Later on we discovered that everybody except us, in our isolated little SNP branch, knew quite well that she was Douglas Heron's mistress. He was a married man, though nobody seemed ever to have met his wife.

Heron was a tall, lean man with a lock of very black hair falling over his forehead. He had a large sharp nose and deep lines in his cheeks which gave him the look of a very emaciated bloodhound. And he had two steel-grey eyes, but with only one of them could he see straight. This was a cool and objective eye, which surveyed the world with uncompromising rigour. But the other's gaze was directed inwards, and no-one else knew what that eye saw.

I began to see quite a lot of Heron in Niamh's company, for in spite of what I had discovered I couldn't keep away from her. Nor did she mind my being around sometimes with herself and Heron: indeed she seemed rather to like it. He was an intelligent man, outwardly pleasant and good company, but I suspected that he was also a cruel one. He had two ways of answering a question which a shy acolyte might put to him on the political scene. Either he would come straight out with the answer, unhesitatingly, as if he had known the question in advance and regarded it with a little genial contempt for its naivety; or else he would wrinkle his nose up and pause for reflection; not indeed to discover the answer, which of course he already knew, but rather to find the right words to make it all clear and simple to a mind less keen and practised than his own. And sometimes a little ghost of amusement would play about his lips, as if he were privy to some esoteric inside knowledge for ever denied to the eager listeners to whom he held forth.

From Tommy and others I picked up a bit about Heron's background. He came from some small town in the north-east of Scotland, maybe Fraserburgh, where his father had been a doctor. During his National Service he had served in Korea and been decorated. Vague rumours flew around about his exploits there, not all of them relating to his undoubted bravery. Then, I learned to my surprise, he had trained for the ministry and completed his divinity degree. But something happened during his year as a probationer which made it clear that he was an unsuitable candidate for the cloth, and he was never ordained. Now he worked at the university in some administrative capacity. He appeared to have plenty of leisure and drove big expensive cars, seeming in fact to have more money than his position might lead one to expect. He was a fanatical nationalist who cared little for the nitty-gritty of grass-roots politics, and he had an explosive temper and a violent streak. Altogether Douglas Heron was an enigmatic man, and perhaps for this reason I felt myself drawn to him.

Others did, too. Not long after Niamh's appearance on the scene we had another new recruit. Derek Greig was one of that race of gingery-headed fanatics, a specimen of which every self-respecting SNP branch was morally obliged to possess in those days. He used to pound the table a lot when making his points and for quite a long time persisted in pretending to spit on the floor whenever the words 'England' or 'English' were used by himself or others. He was an exhausting person to be with, but very well-meaning and likeable, and he had a very nice wife called Mary who was also a member of the branch. Derek was a small, strong, gnome-like figure with a red beard, and worked as a minor civil servant in St Andrew's House. He was also a great proponent of direct action.

Now Tommy and I used to fantasize in a half self-mocking way about possible methods of taking action against symbols of imperialism and repression. The statue of Edward VII in the forecourt of Holyrood Palace, for instance, we saw as a possible target, but the only idea we could come up with for parting the merry monarch from his plinth was somehow to get over the wall at night and tie bands of some kind impregnated with corrosive acid to his ankles. Derek Greig was much more serious. He had very definite ideas about things that could be done, things that were not only quite illegal but also very dangerous and even potentially effective. Moreover, he got Douglas Heron to listen to him and hear him out. Heron paid him the ultimate compliment, it appeared, of taking him seriously, though it couldn't be said that, in my hearing at any rate, he actively encouraged him. He listened, always, with that faint look of superior amusement on his face which was certain not to be noticed by an interlocutor so grimly intent on his own obsessions as Derek was. But he made the odd comment, shrewd and searching always, and that was enough to persuade the iconoclastic rebel that Heron was entirely with him and endorsed all his proposals as realistic and workable.

One lunch-time I was in Sandy Bell's Bar, where I'd half arranged to see Niamh. She did turn up, but Heron happened to be there already, and it quickly appeared that there was some source of tension between them. When they started arguing I tactfully went off a little distance and cracked with other people. There was a big crowd of regulars there that afternoon, including Hamish Henderson surrounded by half-drunk pint glasses, and Finlay Mountsavage holding forth at the bar. Finlay's real name was Bob Dow, but every writer in those days had to have either a *nom de plume* or an impressive middle name which he could use as an adjunct to his surname. Finlay lacked a middle name but his *nom de plume* certainly made up for that lack. He had just been on his way home, as it happened, his wife was waiting for him, but there's mony a slip twixt cup and lip and somehow he found himself turning in to the door of Bell's, and there he was now, well ensconced, and inveighing against the wretched dominance of the nyaff in every aspect of Scottish life. Dermot Taylor was present on that occasion too, I believe – Dermot Taylor who was quite unknown in those days, and as a matter of fact still is, or virtually so.

I was standing around on the fringes of this group, then, making the odd comment but also keeping one ear on what was going on between Heron and Niamh. It appeared that Niamh wanted Douglas to take her as his guest to a big nationalist dinner that was coming up, but Douglas was resisting her because of something to do with his wife – either he had to take his wife to the dinner or he had some other commitment involving her.

It was obviously a kind of test case. The argument went on and on in tones that didn't quite succeed in being hushed, and became more and more heated. Then Niamh suddenly turned away from Heron and said to me, 'Will you take me to the Convention Dinner on Friday, Duncan?' Before I had time to reply, Heron slapped Niamh on the cheek extremely hard, with such a report that everyone in the vicinity stopped talking and turned round in amazement; and, white to the gills, he strode out of the bar without further ado.

Well, I did take Niamh to the Convention Dinner, and later that night I slept with her for the first time, and she taught me things that previously even my most far-fetched daydreams had been innocent of. We were lovers for about a year, but Niamh never ceased to be Heron's lover as well, and indeed primarily so. There was never any doubt about the pecking order. And, yes, I remained content to pick up these crumbs from the rich man's table. – Well, content isn't precisely the *mot juste*, actually. But I won't begin to attempt to describe the torments I went through, because they're not the point.

It was an unspoken rule from the start that Niamh never spoke to me about her relationship with Heron. 'It's something altogether different from you and me': that was the most I could ever get out of her. But she had an awful lot of bruises. And little bits of information filtered back to me. As, for instance, that one time Heron had rung the doorbell of Niamh's flat in Comely Bank when only her flatmate was at home, and asked politely if he could await her arrival. When, about half an hour later, her flatmate heard Niamh let herself in, she was along the corridor in the kitchen; almost immediately she heard a scuffle and then, even before she could react, the front door slamming. Heron had quite effectively beaten Niamh up the instant she had stepped into the sitting room, and was out the door within ten seconds. It appeared to have been an operation planned with military precision.

But she kept coming back to him, for reasons I didn't even try to understand.

Did Heron know of my relationship with his mistress? That was something I never knew for sure. I suspected, naturally, that he did. But most of the time he showed no sign of it. When he did evince hostility, it was invariably by staring at me for a long time with narrowed eyes. At first I found this very disconcerting, but I rather enjoyed flirting with danger, and in the end came almost to appreciate it. Heron was intelligent enough to know, I realized, that he had no more right to Niamh than I did, indeed less, since he was married. And he always liked to keep his cards very close to his chest. We were actually quite friendly, in a strange kind of way, and spent quite a lot of time in each other's company. My strongest memory of him is of how he used to sing Irish rebel songs at nationalist gatherings in a strong, harsh voice, very passionately; and I recall once even seeing tears in his eyes, when he sang of: '*those who died that Eastertide / In the springtime of the year.*'

He used to sing Scottish rebel songs too, but everyone realized in their heart of hearts that, compared with the Irish ones, these bore very little relation to reality, and indeed smacked embarrassingly of braggadocio. But Derek Greig really loved them and got quite carried away when Heron sang, attempting to accompany him in a voice that was sadly lacking in musicality and suggested that he was, in fact, almost entirely tone deaf. Always after such a session the well-oiled gnome would pull Heron away into a corner and engage him in earnest and conspiratorial converse, muttering away relentlessly for what seemed like hours. And Douglas Heron would listen patiently and paternally, with that ironic smile hovering around his mouth, nodding and pursing his lips, and only quite occasionally putting in some shrewd and indispensable comment or *bon mot*.

For all that Heron was nothing if not hard-headed, he had one unexpected oddity in his intellectual make-up: he was a firm believer in metempsychosis. I knew nothing of this until one evening I was in his and Niamh's company at a reading in the New Town Hotel given by the extraordinary Ada Kay, a middle-aged woman from Lancashire who had written a play and believed herself to be a reincarnation of James IV. The reading was organized, I think, by a group called The Heretics – Stuart MacGregor, Willie Neill, Dolina Maclennan, Donald Campbell, John Herdman – that lot. Ada had written a novel called *Falcon* which she claimed was the autobiography of the late lamented monarch, composed by herself out of her memories of this previous life. She was an imposing, Junoesque figure, rather resembling the pictures of Boadicea you used to see in children's illustrated history books. She read very histrionically and with tremendous verve.

After the reading I asked Heron what he had made of it, expecting a taste of his usual amusing, ironical, cynical commentary. But to my astonishment it transpired that – although he had indeed his reservations about this particular case – he took the idea of reincarnation in general entirely seriously; more, he positively believed in it. He discoursed at length about the unsatisfactory ways in which Buddhist tradition reconciled the belief in reincarnation with the denial of the reality of the self. If there was no self, what exactly was it that reincarnated? Various analogies had been proposed, such as that, taking a stack of draughts pieces as an example, each piece, though separate and distinct from all the others, depended upon its predecessors for its position in the stack – or something like that (I probably haven't got it quite right), which at any rate he found unsatisfactory. His preferred metaphor was that of a perennial plant: each year, out of the same root or germ or bulb which contained the genetic material, the plant brought forth new growth and flower, which were distinct from last year's growth but intimately related to it as a new embodiment of the germ's potential. 'The same but different. Or, different but the same,' he summed up in his slightly pompous tone of authority.

Heron had obviously thought a lot about all of this and applied it to a range of matters, personal and cultural. Perhaps it was his old theological bent coming out in a new form. After the Ada Kay reading he reverted to this topic quite frequently. He used often to say, 'One develops in one's own way only after death, only when one is alone.' It was only years later that I discovered by chance that this was not an original remark but a quotation from Kafka; but it seemed to say something about Heron's essential aloneness – and need for that – which was a characteristic one was always aware of, in spite of his surface gregariousness.

Douglas also applied this idea of reincarnation to the case of Scotland. Scotland too could be reincarnated, he believed. He insisted that he didn't simply mean by that a re-birth or renaissance in the usual loose cultural sense – it was a case, rather, of complete death followed by a new appearance in a fresh shape which would, however, be intimately related to that which had preceded it. He expatiated on this idea at great length, sometimes, but it was never really clear to me what, impressive though it sounded, all this could mean in reality.

But the fragile, precarious event in time which had drawn us all together was now coming to an end. Such intangibles always do dissolve, of course, and sometimes there's an exact moment when one becomes aware of the beginning of the end. One evening during a party at Niamh's flat she and Heron disappeared into her bedroom, and the rest of us, maybe half a dozen, had been sitting around talking and drinking for perhaps half an hour when we heard a piercing, rather gruesome shriek – Niamh's – issuing from that quarter. Donald Lumb was there (Le Grand Moan, I used to call him, because he was always complaining about something or other, but only Heron really understood the joke) and, solicitous for Niamh's welfare as ever, he insisted, in the teeth of Alice's contrary and wise advice, on entering that private realm to investigate. He came back very soon and quite sheepishly, and told us that he had found the pair of lovers in an extremely compromising situation which could have borne no possible relation to the impeccable family life of Queen Victoria.

My own affair with Niamh had been rocky for some time and from that day I had nothing more to do with her. Our little group was beginning to disintegrate. Colin defected to Labour as expected, and Cameron the ex-Liberal emigrated to South Africa, a very far from liberal place at the time. Dick Brown got married and gradually stopped coming to meetings. Niamh hung around in Edinburgh for a year or two after taking her diploma, but eventually came to terms with the fact that Heron would never leave his wife for her, and – taking with her that invisible other who walked always at her side – went home to Ireland, where I believe she is now a quite well known artist, and writes poetry too. And a few years after that I got married and settled down, very happily, and now I've taken early retirement from my post as Head of History at the school I taught at for most of my career, and cultivate my garden assiduously. I've always remained friends with Tommy and Alice.

The saddest story is that of wee Derek Greig. He left Edinburgh for the west of Scotland in the early seventies, and quickly got into bad company. He became involved in one of those clandestine nationalist bodies that sprang up around that time, called, I believe, the Sons of Calgacus, which was really dedicated to that direct action after which the fanatical little man had always hankered. A couple of years later he was arrested for conspiracy to violence – a botched attempt to rob a bank – was found guilty and sentenced to a great many years in prison, a substantial number of which he served. I ran into him a couple of years back and he was a sad figure indeed.

As to Douglas Heron – well, there lies a mystery. He just dropped out of the scene, fairly abruptly, not long after Niamh went back to Ireland. The last time I met him was while walking on a beach in East Lothian around 1980. He was friendly enough, but uncommunicative, and looked a lot older, and I didn't even discover where he was living. After that he disappeared altogether; except that Tommy met someone – a fairly reliable informant, apparently – who claimed to have seen him in a café in Amsterdam in the early '90s, talking to a person whom this reliable informant knew to be a British intelligence agent. Make of that what you will. And now some people say that he's dead, and others that he's gone away somewhere, but it's hard to say on what these suppositions are based. Maybe he's out there in Mitteleuropa, or maybe he's already reincarnated and back among us in some unknown form. Or again, maybe he's between lives and developing in his own way, alone, as he always wanted. I like to think that.

And what of the Cause – the Cause, my soul! – for which we were all in our diverse ways working? We called it Independence, or Freedom, but there came along those who wanted to change its name to Home Rule, or Devolution. That's what was settled on in the end, Devolution. And as we patiently awaited Devolution, or something better, people began to die. Stuart MacGregor died, that bonnie balladeer, and the magnificent Fionn Mac Colla, and Sydney Goodsir Smith, and then the great MacDiarmid. When that last happened a shiver went through Scotland, a chill came on the air. But we were awaiting Devolution at that moment, it was just around the corner, consummation was at hand! Then a year later it was 1979, and Devolution disappeared down the drain, and instead we had Mrs Thatcher. So we all put our heids down and got on with whatever else we were doing and tried to forget. And they went on dying. The old warhorses of the SNP died one by one, Arthur Donaldson and Donald Stewart and Robert McIntyre and many another. And the old toothless pit-bulls of the 1320 Club were no more,

Major F.A.C. Boothby and Ronald MacDonald Douglas, and Wendy Wood vanished like snow off a dyke. And still we went on waiting.

And then, after a very long time, what should be on the agenda again but Devolution! But still they went on dying. And now all the bards and writers were disappearing, falling away one by one, Tom Scott and the resplendent Ada Kay and George Mackay Brown up in Orkney and Garioch the canniest of wordsmiths and Jim Annand went the way of all flesh, and the incomparable Sorley MacLean, and Norman MacCaig with all his wit; all these irreplaceable people were gone, and still we were waiting. And a lot of less famous people died too, but now Devolution was once more just around the corner. And my cousin Jean died – the only nationalist in my family apart from myself, and a very staunch one in her own quiet way; Jean died after years of sickness and suffering, and on the morning of her funeral the headline in the *Scotsman* read:

"Power stays with English MPs"
Blair tells Scotland

And of course he was right.

And now we have our Devolution, and the nyaff rules in every corner of Scottish cultural and political life; and the flower of Heron's reincarnated Scotland, struggling up through the mud, is still nowhere to be seen; not yet.

5

Voyaging

On 1 April 1865 the *Fiery Star*, a full built clipper ship of 1360 tons of the Black Ball Line of London, set sail from Moreton Bay, Queensland, the harbourage for Brisbane, bound for Liverpool by the long route round the south end of New Zealand. She had previously been the *Comet* of New York, but the Civil War then raging had resulted in the sale of many such fine ships to foreign owners, and the *Fiery Star* was now in the service of the British Government emigration agency for Queensland, in which capacity she had sailed from Dublin to Moreton Bay the previous September. Her new name was to prove ironically apt.

The ship's manifest showed that she was carrying a full and valuable cargo comprising 2041 bales 3 bags of wool, 134 casks of tallow, 15 bales 2 bags of cotton, 1519 hides, 9013 horns, hoofs and bones, 6 cases of arrowroot, 15 quarter-casks of sherry, 96 cases of cordials, and sundry packages containing among other items colonial woods, bunya-bunyas and natural history specimens. She left

Moreton Bay under the command of Captain W. Hunter Yule – a Scotsman, by the sound of him – with 63 passengers and 42 crew on board.

All went well for the first couple of weeks, and on 11 April the ship was off the south end of New Zealand. Then, seventeen days out, she encountered a severe gale which carried away two of her boats. Two days later, on 19 April, she was in latitude 46° 10' S, longitude 170° W, and running before the wind with a 12-knot breeze, when one of the crew named James Adams noticed smoke issuing from the forecastle. He immediately reported to Capt. Yule, who, with the mate, Mr Sargent, went forward and took the forehatch off, to find smoke coming up in clouds from the lower hold. The hatches were at once battened down; and, the crew responding promptly and vigorously to the crisis, every hatchway in the ship was quickly secured to cut off ventilation. The *Fiery Star* was at this point three to four hundred miles from the Chatham Islands, the nearest land.

The following day, in the teeth of squally gusts, the crew, with the assistance of some of the able-bodied passengers, set to pumping water on the hatches. The stench of burning wool strongly impregnated with arsenic (the spontaneous ignition of which was assumed to be the cause of the fire) had now become insufferable, and the passengers were evacuated from the cabin. Several sails were taken down in an attempt to secure the hatches even further. Up to this point no flames had been seen, and hopes remained that the fire could be kept under until the vessel could make some port in New Zealand. But at 6.00 p.m., in spite of the crew's best exertions, flames broke out through the port bow and the waterways on deck. Capt. Yule, disheartened, decided to give up the attempt to run the ship to land, and began preparations to abandon ship. As a result of the earlier storm, only four of the six boats remained, and in these the captain, all the passengers except one, and most of the crew embarked. But there was not room for all, and sixteen crew members and one passenger volunteered to remain aboard the burning ship. The mate, Mr Sargent, undertook to stay with these men, reportedly saying:

'Well, lads, I'll stick by you, if you'll stick by the ship, and we'll go to work and keep down the fire.'

Capt. Yule took with him the chronometers, chart, sextants and compasses, leaving the chief officer with no means of navigating the ship, which was in flames for'ard when the boats quitted the side of the vessel. Mr Sargent asked them to lie by them for the night and they promised to do so, but on the following morning there was no sign of them. It was supposed that the captain meant to steer for the Chatham Islands.

One of the sixteen crew members left aboard was the 27-year-old ship's butcher, a Scotsman named George Herdman who was a deserter from the British Army. He was the eldest son of an Edinburgh miller and corn merchant, originally from Ford in Midlothian, who had acquired Bell's Mill and Coltbridge Mill on the Water of Leith. George started milling, but was apparently of an ungovernable disposition, and had gone off and joined the army and then deserted. The mill was searched for him when he was hiding there but he escaped detection. His respectable younger brothers then shipped him off to Australia, but he apparently didn't like the experience, and it was in order to get back home that he had signed on as a crew member of the *Fiery Star*.

In those middle years of the nineteenth century the oceans of the world saw the passage of many fugitives and deserters seeking to escape or to find their way back home. With crew members always needed on the countless barques and clippers which plied their way around the globe, it was quite easy for such vagabonds to work their passage without having to answer too many awkward questions about their immediate pasts.

For instance, in August 1876 another Scots skipper, Capt. J. Brown, who commanded a small sailing ship called the *Wandering Chief*, hired in the Javan port of Samarang a seaman calling himself Edwin Holmes, who claimed to have been on a ship named the *Oseco* which had been abandoned in the Indian Ocean earlier that summer. Yet his name never appeared on any list relating to the *Oseco* or to any other ship. Biographical research has proved beyond reasonable doubt that Holmes was in reality the 21-year-old French poet – already, in fact, by this date former poet – Jean-Nicholas-Arthur Rimbaud, who a fortnight previously had deserted, only a couple of weeks after landing in Batavia, from the Dutch Colonial Army with which he had entered into a six-year engagement. Apparently he had spent the intervening time wandering through the jungles of Java before reaching the port of Samarang and signing on with Capt. Brown.

To quote Rimbaud's biographer Graham Robb:

'Rimbaud's ability to gain the sympathy of men in positions of responsibility is well attested. Whoever he was, Edwin Holmes obviously reached a private, illegal agreement with the Captain; when the new crew members were registered in Samarang on 29 August, the day before

The Wandering Chief set sail, Holmes, late of *The Oseco*, was set down as having been taken on by Captain Brown on 11 July, three days before *The Oseco* was abandoned and, perhaps more to the point, over a month before Private Rimbaud was reported missing.' This research confirms a long-ago hunch of the Scottish poet Kenneth White, in a poem whose title refers to an earlier standard Rimbaud biographer, 'What Enid Starkie Didn't Know':

> 'Whit'll be yer name, son?
> – Rimbaud, Arthur
> but I'd rather not sign the register
> – Ach, that'll be nae bother
> we'll pit ye doon as Henderson, Alan
> naebody'll be any the wiser'

Rimbaud's voyage home was not without its excitements: on 30 September, in the South Atlantic in the vicinity of St Helena, very heavy weather with high cross-seas threw the vessel on her beam ends, in which position she remained for thirty hours with hatches and yardarms in the water, until, with six feet of water in the hold, the crew had to cut away mizzenmast and fore and main topgallants. But she survived to reach Queenstown in Ireland on 6 December 1876; and the seaman 'Edwin Holmes' survived too, to continue for a good few years yet his life of restless vagabondage.

That other deserter George Herdman may also have made an attempt, though a feebler one, to conceal his identity, for newspaper reports give his Christian name as 'Richard'; but this could equally have been a mistake. One wonders, at any rate, in what sense he and the other fifteen crew left on board the burning vessel were 'volunteers': perhaps they were really the riff-raff at the bottom of the heap who were for one reason or another considered expendable. But that the mate, Mr Sargent, was genuinely selfless in throwing his lot in with these men and the seemingly doomed clipper can scarcely be doubted. Just as little could doubt be cast on his courage and resolution. No sooner had the boats left the ship than the steam pumps were put into action, and the water from them did something to check the flames. All the blankets and clothes available were used to block up the holes for'ard, and water was pumped on them.

Fortunately at this time the weather was fine, with a moderate breeze. On the 21st they kept a lookout for the boats, but nothing was to be seen of them. Having been without means of navigation all night, Mr Sargent (now Captain *pro tem*) succeeded in getting into the cabin early in the morning and found a compass and chart. The fire was still under but not out. In the afternoon some of the hands set themselves to constructing a raft out of old spars, as a means of escape should the worst come to the worst, and this they completed within a couple of days.

The men realized clearly that their best hope of survival lay in keeping the fire down until they either made land or fell in with a ship, and exerted themselves stubbornly to this end. They had to live entirely on deck, eating the fowls from the hen-coops. They also had to share their living quarters with ten pigs – of which, as ship's butcher, Herdman had perhaps been in charge – as their styes, like most other burnable objects that could be reached, had to be used to keep up the fire for the steam pumps, since it was usually impossible to bring up coals from below because of the gas and steam. In spite of these conditions the men all remained in good health.

Thus it went on for two or three days, with unremitting efforts to keep the fire under control. The decks were cut away in several places to allow water to be pumped down. The foremast had been badly burnt in the way of the cables. On the 25th they encountered very unsettled weather, but kept on sailing NE by N to get in the track of passing ships. That afternoon the pigs, crazed by heat and thirst, ran amok and had to be slaughtered. The squally gales continued until the 28th, by which time the ship was making so much water that she had to be pumped out every two hours. Although there was no sign of smoke when the hatch was taken off on 2 May in an attempt to get coal, there was a great deal of steam and gas, and the heat had increased to such an extent that the pitch was beginning to run out of the seams.

On 4 May, after they had sighted two islands thought to be Mercury and Cuvier, a hole was cut in the deck to get the hawsers up, but they were unable to reach the cables. The ship was labouring a good deal, and around midnight there came a heavy gale, with terrific squalls and rain, and this continued for several days, sometimes with thunder and lightning, and the vessel made a great deal of water. The men had constantly to pump out the ship as well as keeping the steam pumps dousing the fire. In this deplorable condition they sailed on until 11 May, when, at 5.00 p.m. they made land – the East Cape of New Zealand – bearing WSW, distance 26 miles. The *Fiery Star* had sailed some 900 miles in 21 days since the outbreak of the fire. At 10.00 p.m. a ship hove in sight on the lee bow: it proved to be the *Dauntless*, bound for Auckland from Dublin. Captain Moore takes up the story:

> On Thursday, May 11, in latitude 37.5 longitude 175.42 E, my attention was drawn to a vessel firing cannon and rockets, and I immediately put back my main yards. When she came within speaking distance it was found that she was the *Fiery Star*, and was burning. The officer in command asked that a boat might be sent to her, which was at once done. I found the first mate and seventeen hands, the captain, purser, crew and passengers having left her three weeks before, taking all the boats, and leaving the chief officer and the others to their fate. The vessel was in a bad state, her foremast being nearly burnt through. I offered the mate all the assistance that lay in my power. I advised him to stick to the ship, and I would lie by her till the morning, as there might be a chance of getting into harbour with a fair wind. I left one of my life-boats with her. Next morning at nine o' clock I sent a boat to her. The fire was then getting worse. Mr Sargent decided to leave her, but wished me to come aboard to give my opinion before so doing. I went on board and saw that she was getting much worse. I also thought the only thing to be done was to leave her. The mate had done all that man could do to save her. We got off all that we could in the way of provisions, &c., finally leaving her adrift with all hands at 4 p.m. She was then in flames.

The *Dauntless* stood by until 10.30 p.m., when the *Fiery Star*, a beacon on the southern ocean, burned to the water's edge and sank.

The survivors arrived in Auckland on board the *Dauntless* on 15 May. At a meeting of the Auckland Chamber of Commerce tribute was paid to their great bravery and a subscription list was opened for them. In the event the action of the 'volunteers' in remaining on board might almost be attributed to shrewdness as much as to selflessness, for although HM steamship *Brisk* was despatched to try to ascertain whether the boats had reached the Chatham Islands, nothing further was ever heard of Capt. Yule and the more than 80 people he took with him.

As to George Herdman, his life of wandering, like Rimbaud's, was to continue for some years. After he eventually reached home his brothers, in the early 1870s, had him shipped to America, but he again contrived to get home and was immediately shipped out once more. Eventually he came home and was boarded in Orkney, where he lay low until the general pardon of deserters at the time of Queen Victoria's Jubilee in 1887. After that the Fiery Star, as he had come to be known, travelled frequently from Orkney to Edinburgh, all expenses being charged to his brothers at Haymarket Mills (now the wealthiest and most successful flour millers in Scotland), who had to support him on a small allowance all his life. The first intimation that he had arrived was invariably, it was said, a bill for a wreath for his mother's grave, and eventually he would put in an appearance in a cab. When he needed extra money for drink in Orkney (drink had apparently been the cause of his downfall), he would do a day's work as a baker. He never married but, it seems, fathered a considerable illicit progeny. He died and was buried in Orkney in 1905, forty years after his first close encounter with death on board the *Fiery Star*.

Some eight and a half years before those events a much more professional seaman than George Herdman had accomplished the most memorable feat of his career. On 9 December 1856 a meeting of citizens of the town of Ontonagon, Michigan, on the southern shore of Lake Superior west of the copper-mining Keweenaw Peninsula, was organized at a local hotel to honour Captain Redmond Samuel Ryder, master of the propeller *General Taylor*, 462 tons, and his officers. A short time before, Capt. Ryder had braved the tempestuous waters of Lake Superior at a date much later than was normal to bring vital supplies to the communities along the southern shore, notably that of Ontonagon, before the winter ice set in. In fact, it had already begun to do so. The journey was one fraught with great danger, 'a feat no other captain would try', according to the *Lake Superior Miner*.

Ontonagon was isolated from the outside world for five months of the year by the ice, and at this season no supplies could get through by ship and the mail had to be delivered by dog sled. A couple of years previously the people had lived through a 'starving time' which they had survived by slaughtering oxen and eating the corn meal intended for these beasts, and by an emergency trip by local residents to bring back barrels of flour. In 1856 the crisis was caused by the loss on 29 October of the ship which should have brought the last supplies, the *Superior*. As it happened it was the *General Taylor* under Capt. Ryder which had picked up the survivors and retrieved the body of Captain Hiram J. Jones for burial in Detroit.

At the testimonial dinner at the Johnson House the

committee reported a series of resolutions highly complimentary to Capt. Ryder and tendered their cordial thanks to him for the service he had rendered. The resolutions were unanimously adopted, and Capt. Ryder was then presented with a valuable gold watch and chain as a token of the high esteem in which, as seaman and citizen, he was held by the community. The inside back of the watch – a Railroad Timekeeper by E.D. Johnson, London 13902 – was inscribed in an elaborate script:

'Presented to Capt. R.S. Ryder by the Citizens of Ontonagon, L.S., Dec. 9th 1856.'

Redmond Samuel Ryder had been born in Kingston, Ontario, on 12 November 1821, and first shipped as a cabin boy out of Detroit in 1836. He may have come from a family with a seafaring tradition, for his brother George also became a master mariner on the Great Lakes operating out of Detroit. Redmond seems to have sailed in the lower lakes before becoming mate on the schooner *Independence*, master Capt. John Stewart, out of Sault Ste Marie in 1847. He had his master mariner's ticket by 1853; and the following year he married in Sault Ste Marie a 19-year-old widow, Aurelia Sapier, née Bourgeault, who claimed descent from the oldest French stock in the New World. She had been married off very young by her parents, French style, and had lost an infant son as well as her first husband before she met Capt. Ryder. In 1856 Redmond Ryder entered the employment of the Lake Superior Transit Company, and thereafter made his home in Detroit.

A photograph taken in middle age shows a man with a steady gaze, at once shrewd and humorous, and a spade beard and shaven upper lip which make him resemble

Melville's Captain Ahab as portrayed by Gregory Peck. He has a prominent nose and high cheekbones, and the cast of features carries a slight suggestion of native blood, though he was apparently of Manx and Irish descent. He looks like a man who could spin a yarn or two.

The year of Capt. Ryder's marriage witnessed much of the construction of the Sault Ship Canal, which came to be known as the '500 Locks'. This was a revolutionary development for Great Lakes transport, as it allowed ships to carry cargo from the lower lakes through to Lake Superior without having to unload below the rapids. Previously cargo had to be loaded on horse-drawn carts for transit to a boat on Lake Superior. The canal was opened in 1855. In 1862 the first ship through the straits of Mackinac, which divide Lake Michigan from Lake Huron, after the break-up of the ice, and then through the 500 locks, was the *City of Cleveland*, master George Ryder. But the following year the *Water Witch* under George's command foundered in Saginaw Bay, Lake Huron, with the loss of 28 lives including his own. In the same year the *General Taylor*, which Redmond had commanded when he brought the relief supplies to Ontonagon, was lost off Sleeping Bear Dunes in Lake Michigan.

The Great Lakes Shipping Company, also known as J.T. Whiting, and its subsidiary the Lake Superior Transit Company, seem to have had a policy of moving their masters frequently between their various ships. They would have had to anyway, because of the enormous number of losses and fatalities which were incurred every year in the extremely hazardous waters of the lakes. Founderings, collisions and explosions were commonplace occurrences. In 1854, for instance, there were 384 disasters with the loss of 119 lives; in 1856, 597 disasters and 407 lives lost, the total cost of the losses being $3,126,744. These years were far from untypical. Most of the ships commanded at various times by Redmond Ryder came eventually to unhappy ends.

From 1858 to 1861 Ryder was master of the *Mineral Rock*, making many trips to Ontonagon with passengers and supplies, and bringing back copper on the return voyage, including the largest piece of mass copper ever mined and transported up to that date. But in 1862 he was in command of the *Illinois*. On 9 August that year the schooner *Oriole*, which had left the port of Marquette on Lake Superior the previous day with a cargo of iron ore as well as 13 persons including the captain's wife and mother-in-law, entered a blinding fog, but the skipper kept on going. About 3.00 a.m., a steamer 'charged out of the mist', struck the schooner on her starboard quarter and cut the vessel in two. The only survivor was the cook, Andrew Fleming, who spotted the detached stern of the ship, managed to lower its yawl and drifted in it for a day and a half before being picked up. In Marquette, Fleming discovered that his schooner had been downed by the *Illinois* under Capt. Ryder. In the blinding mist of a summer fog, the *Oriole* had unwittingly crossed his bow, and in white-out conditions, the vessels separating immediately after the impact, Ryder was unaware that he had sunk the other. Thinking the schooner not badly damaged, and with considerable injury to the bow of his own vessel, he had continued to Marquette. Two years after this disaster the *Illinois* itself was sunk under a different command.

In the first week of August 1863 Redmond Ryder was

in command of the new propeller *Meteor* on her first trip to Lake Superior. Fortunately she was mastered by another captain when, two years later, she collided with her sister ship the *Pewabic* on Lake Huron due to an error of judgement on the part of the latter's first mate. The *Pewabic* sank within five minutes with the loss of 80 lives. The *Meteor* survived to sail again, but was sunk in 1873 in the Detroit River.

In that same year of 1873 fate finally caught up with Redmond Samuel Ryder after 37 years sailing the Great Lakes, when on 4 December his propeller, the *City of Detroit*, while towing a schooner-barge called the *Guiding Star*, foundered in Saginaw Bay, Lake Huron – where his brother George had perished ten years earlier – with the loss of 20 lives, including those of Ryder himself, his only son John and his nephew John Campbell. The barge and her crew were rescued. Capt. Ryder was seen to remain at his post as his ship went down.

His presentation gold watch did not go down with him, however, and in the year 2000 it was presented by a great-great-grandson, Thomas Ryder Lannon, to the Ontonagon County Historical Society. Redmond Ryder had left behind him, as well as his widow and widowed mother, three daughters. A couple of years after his death his eldest daughter Emma married a young Scottish immigrant from Edinburgh, William Grierson Smith, who happened to be a first cousin of George Herdman, the Fiery Star. Smith went on to make a fortune in the manufacture of varnish, not inappropriately for the son of a furniture auctioneer and the grandson of a cabinet maker. William and Emma Smith's daughter May made several voyages to Scotland in her childhood and youth to visit her father's family, and on one of these she met Bill Macmillan, a tea merchant, and eventually settled in Edinburgh to marry him. Their daughter married another Herdman, the son of a first cousin of both George Herdman and William Grierson Smith; and they became my parents.

So it is perhaps no coincidence that I enjoy a cruise.

6

Cruising

This story's about something that happened to a pal of mine, Wee Davie Cowmeadow his name is, quite a few years back now – and it came straight from his own mouth. Wee Davie has a business refurbishing old bits and pieces of furniture – you couldn't really call it restoring – and he regards doors as his speciality. Trouble is, Davie's joinery skills are pretty minimal, and he's always had to rely on a string of joiners to help him out in their spare time whenever there's anything needing done that requires a bit of expertise. And that gets him into all kinds of difficulties.

That's the way it was this time when Davie had a door to deliver to a very good address in the New Town. Young Stuart, the current joiner, should have been with him to fit the handles, which he was to get hold of at his work; but young Stuart couldn't make it that evening. He'd had to take his pregnant sister to the hospital with high blood pressure – or so he claimed. Emergency, like. Not only that, but Davie's mate, Bill, had been in a punch-up a couple of nights before, and what with that and a hangover, he'd taken a day off his work, and as a result the door hadn't been taken out of the vat in time to be finished. But the customer – Sir Hamish Cadfoot, the well known QC – was really agitating for the job to be done, so Davie thought he'd better just take the door round anyway and come back later with young Stuart to finish it off.

So Davie goes off to the New Town with Bill, who's got a black eye, and rings the bell. Sir Hamish comes to the door looking awfae glum.

'You said you'd give me advance warning!' he bawls him out.

So Davie has to make out he didn't have the number, and Sir Hamish says he's given it to him three times; and then Davie has to explain about young Stuart not being able to come, and how Bill's just out of his bed with the flu, and how the door isn't finished but they'll hang it for him now and come back next week and give it a bit sand and a couple of coats of white vinegar. And Sir Hamish isn't very happy with any of this at all, but there's not a lot he can do about it.

But then, when they try to fit the door, they find it's too big, and Davie tells Sir Hamish he's given him the wrong measurements. At that the advocate really flies off the handle, if that's the right expression in the circumstances.

'Cynthia!' he yells to his wife. 'Bring me the tape measure!'

And in comes Lady Cadfoot with the tape measure, a pretty smart piece and very well preserved, but her face is all blotchy and it's obvious she's been greetin'.

So they argue to and fro about whose fault it is, but the

bottom line is that they'll have to take the door back to the shop.

'Young Stuart'll be down at the beginning of next week, sir,' says Davie, 'an' he'll cut the door back . . . Let's see now . . . he plays pool on a Monday . . . We'll get it tae ye Tuesday – no, better make it Wednesday, sir. Wednesday, that's definite.'

But oh no, that's no good for Sir Hamish, they're going off on holiday and they won't be wanting all that disruption on the eve of their departure.

'Ay, well,' comes back Davie, 'we're off frae the Friday wursels, sir. Trades holidays, like.'

And Davie's wishing he was off on that cruise already, the cruise to the northern capitals on the *Saturn* from Leith, that he's won in the 'Spot the Ball' competition in the *Evening News*. Anyway they agree that it'll have to wait till the end of the month, and Davie's in such a hurry to get out of the place that off they go without the door, so they have to come back, and Davie overhears the lady saying something about a 'hopeless little man'. And by this time he's so flustered that in manoeuvring the door out of the drawing room they knock this Chinese vase off a table and smash it to smithereens. Davie says he's sorry at once, of course, but Lady Cadfoot goes into complete hysterics.

'Mummy's vase!' she bawls, greetin' her eyes out. 'It was priceless! You clumsy bloody oafs!' And on and on she rages, while Sir Hamish just shakes his head in despair.

'Insurance'll cover it, like . . . ' tries the wee man. He can be pretty gallus, Davie.

Anyway, the trades holidays come along at last and

Davie can forget it all for a week or two. And as the *Saturn* pulls away from Leith, headed for Oslo, Stockholm, Copenhagen, Hamburg and Amsterdam, there he is parading about on deck in his blazer and cravat and his yachting cap. And he sees this couple leaning over the rail discussing the islands of the Forth, there's something familiar about the voices, and as he's about to wander past them the man turns his head, and it's Sir Hamish Cadfoot. He looks away again quickly, but Davie steps right up and slaps him on the shoulder.

'So this is where you go for yer holidays! Turn-up for the books, eh?'

Sir Hamish is pretty taken aback, naturally, but he does his best, and Davie explains how he's won the trip in 'Spot the Ball'. And immediately Lady Cadfoot asks if he's brought his wife with him.

'Naw, naw,' says Davie. 'See, my wife's went aff, last year there, she's puntin' about wi' a taxi-driver . . . so I'm fancy-free.'

So they chat a bit, and it turns out that Sir Hamish isn't too well and the doctor's recommended some sea breezes.

'Aw, I'm sorry to hear that . . . What's the trouble, like?' asks Davie with his usual tact.

At this Sir Hamish turns all lofty and remote and implies that his condition is so rare that Davie couldn't possibly have heard of it. But in the end he can't resist the temptation to talk about it.

'It's known as postural-sacral redundancy syndrome, actually,' he says grandly.

'Get away! That's what my auntie had . . . the very same!'

Sir Hamish reacts to this with complete incredulity, but Davie rattles off chapter and verse, asks him if there's epiglottal involvement and tells him that in his auntie's case it was into the cerebellum.

'Ay! I mind when she tellt my Uncle Hughie: "I've got posterior-sacral redundancy syndrome, Hughie." My uncle says, "Ay!" he says. "That means if ye sit on yer arse all day, yer legs'll eventually drap aff!" He was trying to cheer her up, like . . .

'So the doctor's recommended sea air, eh?' Davie goes on after a bit of a silence.

'He thought it might keep me going for a bit yet,' Sir Hamish responds jocularly.

'Ay, even if ye get anither year or two, like, that'll always be somethin', eh?'

Lady Cadfoot seems really miffed at this and protests that the doctors are all confident that the treatment Sir Hamish is getting will be effective.

'Ay, that's what they tellt my auntie,' says Davie. 'Mind you, she was an older person than yersel . . . I'm sorry, am ah speakin' outa turn?'

And, judging by the consternation on their faces, he was indeed. So Davie thinks it's time to skedaddle. But after he's unpacked his case he comes back on deck, and there's Sir Hamish still leaning over the rail, looking really dejected, but no sign of Cynthia. Davie joins him and this time Hamish is quite chatty, and admits to Davie that he and Cynthia have had a flaming row. Davie puts on his sympathetic face, and the lawyer really opens up and starts waxing sentimental about the beauties of Scotland and how sad he is to be leaving home. Then Davie takes up the theme and goes on about how he was taking a stroll near Perth the other weekend on a beautiful sunny afternoon. Davie's got quite a way with words when he sets his mind to it.

'I got a glisk, like,' he explains, 'juist a wee view ye understand, of a' these white towers shinin' faur away in the sun through this gap . . . I'm tellin' ye, Hamish,' – they were on first name terms by this time – 'it was that clear, it was that beautiful, it coulda been the towers of Camelot.'

'How splendid! What was it, David?'

'It wis Dundee, 's a matter of fact. Ninewells Hospital. But there ye are.'

And Sir Hamish tells him how evocative his description was, and how much he enjoys Davie's company, and what a lot they're going to have to talk about in the dining saloon.

'You know we're sitting at the same table? No? Well, that's what I had the row with Cynthia about, actually. She was going to refuse to sit with you . . . the vase, you understand. But I insisted. And I'll tell you something else,' he says, lowering his voice confidentially. 'I was actually jolly pleased when you smashed that vase. I've always hated it.'

'Ach, well,' says Wee Davie with a modest air, 'dae wur best, ken.'

So that night at dinner Davie finds himself in the company of the Cadfoots and a really prosy minister called the Reverend James Arbuthnot. And after the minister had finished saying a really mammoth grace, they began introducing themselves. And the minister, who was slightly deaf, thought that Sir Hamish's name was 'Catfood', which was pretty embarrassing, so Davie told a funny story about the origin of the name Cowmeadow, but it didn't seem to go down all that well. But then Sir Hamish ordered some wine and they all loosened up a bit, and the Rev. Arbuthnot sighed and told them all how he was on the cruise to help him recover from the death of his wife. And Cynthia, not to be outdone, bored on to the minister about how ill her husband was. Then they had an argument about the meaning of the word 'terminal', with Sir Hamish, who was a stickler for correct language, telling Davie he'd got it all wrong; but Cynthia took Davie's side, and it was obvious that the Cadfoots weren't getting along too well together.

And before long Davie begins to get the sense that Cynthia's flirting with him a bit, no doubt mainly to get up Hamish's nose; and the wee man thinks to himself, well, what about it? Why not take up the challenge?

'Saltimbocca with shallots in a nutmeg sauce? Mmm!' trills the lady, reading the menu. 'I do adore shallots!'

'Ay,' says Davie, 'think we'll ca' ye the Lady of Shallots!'

'Oh, Davie, that's disgraceful!' she laughs coyly. 'I see you're a punster, in addition to all your other talents.'

And he sees she's impressed, so he decides to put on a bit of a show for her. Now Davie's something of an expert on theology, believe it or not. He's one of the great army of Scottish autodidacts. And now he comes right out and asks the minister his opinion on the subject of the *Theotokos* – 'The Godbearer – the Mother of God, like.' A tough nut for a Protestant minister to crack, that one.

Arbuthnot, of course, is completely taken aback – as who wouldn't be? – and Davie sees his chance and gets tore right in. First of all he gets the minister to agree that Jesus is true God.

'Right, Jim, Jesus is God an' Mary's his Maw, excuse ma French, so Mary's the Mother of God. Am I right or am I wrang?'

'Ah now, hold on, David, hold on. In Our Lord Jesus Christ there are two natures, human and Divine. Now as to the human nature, the Virgin Mary is undoubtedly his mother. But as to the Divine—'

'Ay, now we're gettin' tae it, Jim. Two natures but one Person, Jim. Am I right or am I wrang? Two natures but one Person, OK?'

The man of the cloth's utterly nonplussed and bamboozled.

'Yes, yes, that is indeed the true position,' he has to admit.

'Right then. Way I see it, a wumman can only be the mother of a person, she cannae be the mother of a nature – disnae make sense, that. So she's the mother of a person, an' that person – as ye've admitted yersel, Jim – is God. So Mary's the Mother of God. *Quod erat demonstrandum*, excuse ma French.'

And Davie sits back and folds his arms triumphantly, and the minister can only stutter and can't come up with a word to say in reply. And needless to say the Cadfoots are completely gobsmacked; they've never heard anything like this in their lives. And now Davie plays his trump card. He totally changes the subject and asks Cynthia if by any chance she's a granny – which he knows fine she is, as he's already heard her going on about their 'little Samson', the apple of their eye.

'Right, then,' he says. 'You are the candidate chosen

by this table, Cynthia – I think we can a' agree – to be our entrant for the Glamorous Grannies Competition. To be held on Thursday evening in the Blue Lounge there. I seen it on the noticeboard.'

'Oh, Davie!' she cries, beside herself with delight, 'don't be ridiculous! I couldn't possibly!'

'Jim, I appeal to you! Did you ever see a granny mair glamorous than this yin?'

'Well now, David, you are putting me on the spot. Chivalry demands that I say No. And No I do say, not because chivalry demands it, but because it is true.'

'There ye are then! You cannae refuse the minister.'

'You're all so persuasive!'

Sir Hamish, need I say, has been gnashing his teeth listening to all of this.

'At the risk of putting a damper on all this ardour,' he pontificates, 'I agree with you, Cynthia, that it would scarcely be appropriate.'

'Oh, I know that you don't consider me glamorous!'

'Cynthia, that is scarcely the point—'

'I notice that you don't deny it, though!'

Well, they go on arguing the toss about it, but it's obvious from the start that Hamish is on a hiding to nothing. Cynthia's really got the bit between her teeth, and the best Hamish can do is to attempt a dignified retreat.

'I see there is nothing I can do to prevent you, Cynthia, if you are determined. You will have to forgive me if I absent myself from the great occasion.'

'Oh, I shall put a brave face on it. But my two good friends will be there to support me?' And she looks at Davie and the minister for confirmation.

And of course they were. And what's more, she won.

And from that point on it seemed that Davie couldn't put a foot wrong with Cynthia.

So they run into each other on the deck the morning after the Glamorous Grannies, and Cynthia tells Davie that she owes it all to him that she is coming out of the shadow of her sense of worthlessness, in which she has been shrouded for a quarter of a century, thanks, needless to say, to Hamish. And Wee Davie knows just how to play it.

'Cynthia, you are a very lovely lady. You can be confident that I speak in all sincerity when I say that you have no valid grounds for considering yourself worthless.'

'Oh, thank you! Thank you, Davie! You understand so much. Davie, we must never let Hamish discover what happened in Oslo.'

'Eh? What was that, then? It's a' a bit hazy, like—'

'Oh, Davie, you know! You can't fool me. We both know, don't we? Not that we did anything wrong. Still, it was there, wasn't it?'

'Oh ay, Cynthia. It was there a' right.'

Then she hesitates for a moment . . .

'Davie, Hamish is *dying*. Oh, what am I saying, Davie? Oh! Here he comes!'

And along comes Hamish looking really woebegone, and immediately starts talking about his illness, and how awful he feels, and Cynthia gets more and more impatient and tells him to be more positive: the sun is shining, it's a wonderful day and they're sailing through breathtaking scenery, and soon they'll be in Copenhagen, and so on and so forth. But the effect of this is only to set Hamish more firmly on his high horse:

'I'm sure the day must seem wonderful the morning

after one has been declared the most glamorous grandmother on board the good ship *Saturn*. My situation is far otherwise. Dr Malcolm Fraser, consultant physician, has told me . . . '

At this Cynthia goes right off the deep end:

'Oh, he's going to start talking about his horrible boring syndrome again! I can't bear it, Hamish, I just can't bear it . . . Oh, I can't trust myself to say any more!' And off she storms.

And once more Davie and Sir Hamish find themselves leaning on the rail together.

'You see what I have to put up with, Davie.'

'Women are a' the same, Hamish.'

'Yes, it must have been awful for you when Marlene went off with that taxi driver.'

'Ach, well. You have to be philosophical about thae things, eh, Hamish? She'd got awfae thick in the leg an' a', Marlene. But it was a blow awright.'

'But you came through, Davie. You survived.'

Then Sir Hamish gets really confidential and tells Davie that he's never had many friends – real friends, that is. But he knows Davie has a deep understanding of the way he's feeling. And he tells him how he's been what's called a success in life: he's respected in his career – tipped for higher things, even – he has a beautiful wife, children of whom he is quietly proud, and now a lovely grandchild. 'Little Samson, you know.' And he has never known material want. And he's taken it all for granted. And life seemed to be proceeding on its predetermined track. Then one day one doesn't feel too good, just in a vague way, nothing you can put your finger on, but one thinks it best to go to the doctor. Tests follow and suddenly there he is, staring you straight in the face: the one you've never wanted to think about, even to acknowledge, saying, 'Here I am, right beside you, very, very close, coming for you soon.' *Death.*

'The Grim Reaper, eh, Hamish? Comes tae us a'.'

'Yes – you understand, don't you, Davie? You have an insight into these things. If only Cynthia could see it as you do!'

'Way I see it, Hamish, Cynthia's denying your illness. Disnae want tae face it, like. She's angry with the syndrome, see, but you cannae really be angry wi' a syndrome, it cannae answer back. So she's angry wi' you instead, for having the syndrome. Awright? Ye get my meaning?'

'Perfectly! Perfectly! It fits! Davie, you're a very remarkable person . . . '

So now Davie finds himself, willy-nilly, the confidant of both the Cadfoots. And the next thing that happens is that the Rev. Arbuthnot, who's an observant man and well aware of this whole situation – and also an interfering one who can't keep his nose out of other folk's business – takes Davie aside and suggests that he should act as a go-between to effect a reconciliation between man and wife at this sad juncture in their lives! And this is all a bit too much for the wee man. In fact, it sends shivers up and down his spine! But the minister has a persuasive way with him.

'David,' he sermonizes, 'Hamish and Cynthia are running away from their feelings. They are seeking through confrontation to defend themselves from the onslaught of the intolerable. They must be brought to understand that only through facing their pain – facing it and sharing it together – will it be possible for them to overcome it, to triumph over it. They need to be helped, David, they need to be shown the way. What do you say?'

'I'm no up tae it, Reverend, honest.'

'But you are, David,' he insists. 'Just rely on your instincts – you have an unusually fine gift of intuition. You have been given the opportunity to be a reconciler, David, a peacemaker. That is a very rare privilege.'

Davie capitulates. 'When you put it like that, Jim, I cannae refuse.'

'Excellent man!' enthuses Arbuthnot, and shakes him warmly by the hand. 'By the way, David, if you don't mind me asking, how did you become so very proficient in theology?'

'Ach, well,' says Davie. 'I used tae work as a barman, like.'

By Copenhagen, which is their next port of call, Cynthia's making her designs on Wee Davie pretty plain, and Davie's all mixed up. He wants to try his luck with her, of course, but he's sorry for Hamish too, and on top of that there's his solemn undertaking to the Rev. Arbuthnot. And Cynthia's never done going on about how awful Hamish is, and how Davie's helping her overcome her sense of worthlessness and realize her untapped potential. She even starts calling him her 'little alchemist' who's changing her base metal into gold. So they're sitting at a pavement café waiting for Hamish to join them, and drinking schnapps, and Cynthia starts quizzing Davie about his ex-wife.

'What was she like? Marlene? Tell me about her.'

'See that Little Mermaid we seen this morning? Marlene was the very opposite o' that. Marlene's a fish from the waist up!' And Davie roars with laughter at his own joke.

'Oh, Davie, you are an idiot!' trills Cynthia. 'Tell me more.'

'No much mair tae tell, Cynthia. We were married nine year. Nae kids. Then she went aff wi' a real foul taxi driver ca'd Tommy Slattery. That's about it, ken.'

'Has there been anyone else, Davie?' she asks, edging closer. 'Since Marlene left, I mean. I'm not trying to pry.'

Like hell, thinks Davie, all embarrasssed. 'Ach, well, juist a wee bit romp here an' there. Nothin' serious, ken.'

'If there had been someone else, where would I have been? Without my little alchemist! My strong, handsome little alchemist . . . Oh, Davie!'

'C'moan, darlin', gie's a break!' says Davie, looking over his shoulder apprehensively. 'Hamish could walk round that corner any minute.'

But there's no stopping her now. Next she's telling him that she and Hamish haven't had sex since the appearance of the 'syntroms of the symbrome' – the lady's pretty well on by this time, and so's Davie for that matter.

'Davie,' she wheedles, 'I don't know how to say this. We haven't known each other much more than a week – I mean, really known each other . . . Oh, Davie, Davie, I want to feel your strong arms around me!'

And just at that moment, right on cue, up comes Sir Hamish. He's all footsore and weary after walking about Copenhagen for hours, trailing round museums and getting himself lost. And he arrives to find his wife and Wee Davie completely drunk and obviously getting on like a house on fire. By this time Davie's even singing 'Wonderful, wonderful Copenhagen'. So it's not surprising that the poor guy's a bit frosty.

'I admire that woman,' Davie straight away breenges in to him, quite oblivious. 'Speakin' personally, that is a very wonderful woman. An' I mean that very sincerely, Hamish . . . 'Scuze me, ah'm drunk.'

'Really? How interesting. I've always wanted to meet someone who was drunk.'

'Oh, he's arrived all right, hasn't he, Davie?' says Cynthia, spoiling for a fight. 'Mr Smartypants has arrived!'

'The most fuckin' wonderful woman in the whole fuckin' world . . . Am ah speakin' outa turn?'

'You've made your point, Davie. Cynthia is the most wonderful woman in the world. That's agreed. Just for the sake of argument. Let's leave it at that. OK?'

'What a shit you are, Hamish!'

'No offence, Hamish!' puts in Davie desperately. 'Awright? Nae offence! Put it there, pal. Greatest pal ah've ever had in ma life. 'S a matter of fact baith of yous is ma pals. Know what wad gie me very great pleasure?' he carries on, thinking of the Rev. Arbuthnot and his mission. 'Tae see the baith o' ye's in harmony wi' wan anither . . . ' – and he attempts to put his arms round both their shoulders.

'Oh, boak!' says Cynthia, furious. And suiting the action to the word, she's promptly sick on the pavement.

'Oh, good Lord!' cries Hamish in despair. 'Why am I here? Why did I come on this cruise? Why was I ever born? Never mind, I'll be dead soon.'

And Davie has to get the pair of them back to the boat in a taxi.

Well, the wee man's up to his oxters in trouble now. Cynthia's making a dead set at him, she's all engorged with lust, Hamish still wants him to be his confidant, but he's a bit suspicious at the same time, and the minister's breathing down Davie's neck, nagging on at him all the time about his 'office of mercy' to their dear friends. And the only person Davie has to confide in is Sonia, the barmaid on the boat, an English lass, whom he's been chatting up a bit on the side.

'Mair trouble, Sonia. Yon minister's got me working as a marriage guidance counsellor – for the Cadfoots, like. And here's me tryin' to get away frae that Cynthia, oot o' her clutches, ken. I'm no' up tae it, Sonia, honest I'm not. I'm juist an ordinary sort o' boy – no' intae that kind o' stuff.'

'You underestimate yourself, Davie,' says Sonia. 'I'm sure you could cope with Lady Cadfoot, no problem.'

'It's no' juist that, Sonia. See, her man's dyin' like, posterior-sacral redundancy syndrome, I cannae dae that tae him on his deathbed.'

But Sonia's thinking maybe she can come in for a cut if Davie gets his hands on the Cadfoot money, and she's quite a persuasive kind of girl. So she tells him that after Hamish is dead Cynthia's going to need consoled, and if she doesn't get it from Davie then she's going to be looking elsewhere. But if Davie is around he's going to land on his feet – won't get another chance like that in his lifetime! Davie hasn't given a thought to the money up till now – he's not really a mercenary sort – but this does give him pause. So he cogitates for a minute or two.

'Did you ever hear o' a boy ca'd Peter Abelard, Sonia? Lived in the twelfth century. Great poet, great thinker, great lover. Revolutionized morality, Peter Abelard. Said that sin was a' in the intention, like. Ken what I mean?'

'No.'

'Right. Let's suppose I'm a married man, Sonia, an' I'm on this boat an' I'm on ma way tae ma cabin for the night, get ma heid doun, OK? An' suddenly there's a power cut.'

'Not very likely, Davie. We've got our own generator, you know.'

'Naw,' says Davie, 'but juist for the sake of argument, like. C'mon, Sonia, anything can happen in a storm. So, the lights are oot. I gaes in an' gets intae bed and makes love tae my wife. Only, it's no my wife, it's you.'

'It's me, Davie?'

'Ay. Juist for the sake of argument, like. Adultery, you might think? Nae way. Peter Abelard comes along: no, he says, the boy didnae commit adultery. See Wee Davie there, he says, he thought he wis makin' love tae his wife, so he didnae intend tae commit adultery. An' if he didnae intend tae dae it, then really speakin' he didnae dae it. Revolutionized morality, that.'

'So you reckon that gives you the go-ahead with Lady Cadfoot, do you?' asks Sonia, a bit sceptical about this line of argumentation.

'Well, see, way I look at it, Sonia, I dinnae intend tae dae nothin' wrong wi' Cynthia. An' if I dinnae intend it tae happen, nae herm, eh?'

And even if Davie wasn't entirely convinced by his own logic, he'd at least succeeded in persuading himself that it wasn't time to give up on Cynthia just yet.

That evening, in the dining saloon, the sniping between the Cadfoots was carrying on worse than ever. Cynthia seemed pitilessly determined to put Hamish down at every available opportunity, and if one wasn't available then she somehow managed to create it. And old Hamish gave as good as he got. All this was a terrible reflection, of course, upon Davie's efforts as an angel of mercy, and the minister kept sighing and casting meaningful looks in his direction. Eventually Arbuthnot went so far as to make a guarded reference to the obligations entailed by the marriage vow 'in sickness and in health', at which point Hamish started crying shamelessly. And it was just at that moment that the jovial Captain Lindqvist strode up to our group's table.

'So! Our happy party! I think you all have wonderful times on this voyage.'

'Is it that obvious?' says Hamish in a stage whisper.

'I come to communicate glad tidings!' beams the captain. 'The results of the General Knowledge Quiz are now available, and I am happy to say, Mr Cowmeadow, that you are the winner! So – you have won a half-gallon bottle of Scotch whisky, and with it goes the title *Brain of the Boat!* Congratulations, Mr Cowmeadow! First, *Spot the Ball* winner, now *Brain of the Boat!*'

'Oh Davie, that's wonderful!' shrieks Cynthia, clapping her hands. 'What a talented lot we are, aren't we – Glamorous Grannies and Brains of the Boat! Davie, you're quite a man.'

'No bad for an ordinary boy that left school at fifteen, eh?'

'And the runner-up, too, is of the party!' continues the captain. 'Well done, Sir Hamish. Now. I have a little proposal. As you know, tonight after dinner we have Grand Ball. On this voyage, I hope that we have an innovation. It depends on you. Before commencement of the Ball, in a little ceremony we crown the King and Queen of the good ship *Saturn*. After the coronation, the Royal couple will lead off the dancing – the first waltz. That is all. Now, who better to be our King and Queen than our Brain of the Boat and our most exceptionally Glamorous Granny? What say you to my proposal? I am in your hands.'

And naturally the proposal is greeted ecstatically by Cynthia, and by Wee Davie with his usual genial insouciance.

'How privileged I feel to be sitting at this royal table!' offers Arbuthnot graciously when the captain has departed.

'I suppose it would be quite useless for me to protest,' says Hamish after an eloquent silence.

'I was waiting for it. I was just waiting for it. All right, Hamish, make your protest. We are listening.'

'If the inexpressible vulgarity of the whole thing isn't obvious to everyone, then there is little point in my saying anything.'

'The inexpressible vulgarity! Well, excuse me! If His Lord High Wetblanketship says so, it must be right!'

'Cynthia, if you want to make a degrading public spectacle of yourself that is your concern. I have registered my protest and my conscience is clear.'

'You're a snob and a wimp, Hamish – a snob and a *wimp!*'

'I shall say no more. I shall not be there to witness this crowning folly.'

'Well, what an absolutely crushing blow! Davie, can we possibly be crowned in Hamish's absence? I mean, would it even be legal?'

'Dinnae ask me, Cynthia. Ah'm keepin' outa this – ma hands are clean.'

And then the minister decides to intervene. Big mistake.

'Well, I must say, this is most distressing,' he puts in. 'Just a few minutes ago we were all so happy.'

'You keep out of this, you prating old faggot!' yells Cynthia, quite beside herself. 'Keep your moralizing for your sermons!'

And with that she grabs Wee Davie by the arm and drags him, protesting feebly, out of the dining room.

Now picture the scene in the ship's bar two or three hours later. The ball's over and Davie and Cynthia, wearing their crowns and both completely pie-eyed, are sitting in front of an already well-breached half-gallon bottle of whisky. Sonia whispers to Davie not to drink too much and mess it all up, but the wee man assures her he's in full control. Now Cynthia's got her arm round his neck and she's whispering sweet nothings in his ear.

'Oh, I could have danced all night! Davie, isn't it a night for clichés? It's just all been so magical. I feel I've shed thirty years in three hours. Don't you feel the same?'

And Davie responds in song:

'When you are in love / It's the loveliest night of the year . . . '

Then she starts telling him about how she fell in love at the League of Pity Ball in the Assembly Rooms all those years ago and had a passionate, tempestuous romance, and at first Davie thinks she's talking about old Hamish, but it turns out to be some twit called Marcus Waddell-Farr.

'Tell me about *your* youth, Davie. Was there any romance with that kind of quality – you know, that special something extra that seems as if it's not quite of this world?'

'Eh, well . . . ' says Davie, frowning and thinking hard, 'there was that wee bird I done down the Isle o' Man, right enough . . . '

And now Cynthia's on about how they're doomed lovers, the pair of them, Tristan and Isolde, Abelard and Eloise, Dante and Beatrice . . .

'No, no! You are Count Vronsky, and I am Anna Karenina, that's it! I often used to be told I was like Greta Garbo!'

'Greta Garbo, eh? I get tellt I'm like Rab C. Nesbitt.'

By this time Sonia's closing the bar, and Cynthia's telling Davie not to drink any more because they've got important business to attend to in his cabin.

'Davie, Davie!' she's slobbering into his ear, 'I want you, I want you, I want to feel you inside me, now, I can't wait!'

'Ach, I know, Cynthia, I want you an' all – it's Hamish I'm thinkin' aboot, darlin'. See, Hamish is ma pal . . . I cannae dae that tae my pal, an' him dyin' an' that . . . It widnae be right, darlin' – he'll no be wi' us much longer. Can we no juist wait till he's deid, Cynthia?'

'Oh, you precious moralist! Come on, Davie, we're going.'

And off she drags the wee man, vainly protesting, to his cabin. But exactly what did or didn't happen there I never could get Davie to say in so many words.

So the next incident I do know about is when Davie and his pal Hamish are drinking together the following night in a bar in the notorious Reeperbahn in Hamburg. No place for the ladies, and the Rev. Arbuthnot, after evincing a fleeting interest in 'savouring the bright lights', as he put it, has chickened out on the excuse of wanting to keep an eye on Cynthia, who 'appeared to be unwell'.

'Ay, that's the soft underbelly of the Scottish macho culture for ye, Hamish.'

'Indeed,' says Sir Hamish. 'Well, we're just going to have to get drunk, Davie, you and I . . . Davie, I think we should have a talk, you know. I think you and I have a great deal to talk about, Davie.'

Davie can only nod warily, and Hamish settles himself down for a lengthy discourse. And he talks of the approach of death, of how it makes one ask oneself what exactly is important in life and what isn't. What in one's wretched little life has enhanced it and lent it dignity? As the darkness closes in one finds oneself confronted with these questions; one asks oneself what things have had that quality, that value. Career? No, at the end of the day no more than a job well done. Material possessions? Even less so. One's family? Right, now we're getting somewhere. Hamish would like to see little Samson growing up, perhaps enjoy the pleasure of more grandchildren. Family love – a simple thing. And at every point Hamish looks to his hapless drinking companion for confirmation.

From there it is natural to pass to the deeper bond, the love and trust that exist between husband and wife. Significant looks. But there's something else that goes hand-in-hand with family love, complements it, rounds it out as it were. Yes: we're talking about friendship. And what are the qualities that make friendship real? Tolerance. Frankness. Give-and-take. And loyalty – trust. Yes, that's the bottom line.

'Trust. So simple. Don't you agree, Davie?'

'Ay, ye're right there, Hamish. There's truth in that.'

'You and I, Davie, we're friends, aren't we? Our friendship has these qualities, doesn't it? Frankness, for instance, loyalty, trust? I think it has those?'

'Put it this way, Hamish – you're the greatest pal I've ever had – no kiddin'!' says the wee man desperately. 'I mean that very sincerely. Greatest pal I've ever had in ma hale fuckin' life – put it there, pal!'

And Davie extends his hand to be shaken; but all the expansive bonhomie has departed from Sir Hamish's countenance and he just stares coldly at the terrified wee man.

'Don't give me that, Davie. I know what happened last night.'

Silence. Davie hangs his head for a long moment.

'Nothin' happened, pal, honest. See, the way it was, Hamish . . . ken, the whisky – distiller's droop, an' that? Nothin' happened, pal. Honest.'

'Really?' says Hamish, looking surprised but interested. 'You don't mean to tell me? Well . . . That won't get you off the hook. The sin lies not in the action but in the intention. Peter Abelard, you know – don't you? Still, never mind. I've always wanted to be cuckolded, all my married life.'

'I've tellt ye, Hamish – *nae*thing *happ*ened!'

'Well, well, I'm not one to bear a grudge. Cynthia was in need of a good shafting. Just a pity she didn't get it, that's all. Come on, let's have another drink.'

'Ay, let's dae that, Hamish. Nae offence, pal, OK? Put it there . . . '

And this time the proffered paw is accepted. But the truce feels to Davie like an uneasy one, and his suspicions are not long in being justified, for quite without warning Hamish kicks him viciously on the ankle under the table. Poor Davie starts blubbering with the shock.

'I never meant nothin' tae happen wi' Cynthia, Hamish, honest,' he whines. 'That's why Wee Davie drank sae much whisky, so's he couldnae get it up! So ye see, pal, the intention wisnae there!'

'Davie – is this really true?'

'Ay! Wee Davie drank that much whisky so's he widnae betray his pal . . . and then' (and he starts to blubber again) 'his pal kicked him!'

Then they fall on each other's shoulders and Hamish calls himself a mean, despicable swine and they swear to be pals for ever.

'Oh, Davie, I've been such a wretch, but the strain I've been under – to face death and betrayal together! This is the end, Davie: I think I shall die tomorrow – perhaps even tonight. Oh, but Davie,' he sobs pitifully, 'I don't want to die in Germany!'

'Better get back to the ship, eh?'

'Yes, yes . . . Davie, if I don't make it back, kiss Cynthia for me just once! No, no, kiss her again and again! Take her, Davie, she's yours for ever, I deliver her into your hands!' the advocate raves.

'Are ye sure about that, Hamish?'

'Yes, yes, I'm sure. I've just won a great victory in my soul, Davie – I give Cynthia into your hands, my friend – take her . . . '

'Well, if you're sure that's a' right – ye'll no regret it, Hamish, I'll look after her, pal—'

'A great weight has been lifted from my mind . . . But my strength is failing fast, Davie. Help me to a taxi, my friend!'

And off they stagger.

You can imagine that the next morning at breakfast, as they're approaching Amsterdam, there's two pretty woebegone faces. But Cynthia's feeling fine. She's fully recovered by now from the Grand Ball and its aftermath, and she's thoroughly enjoying the discomfiture of the two men, making sly asides to the minister and really sticking the knife in where it hurts most.

'So how did you find the famous Reeperbahn, boys? All that jazz, the lurid night life, the risqué clubs, the sleazy brothels – did you do manly and virile things in the Reeperbahn, you dissolute pair of roués?'

'Naw, naw, Cynthia, we done nothin' like that, honest, we juist got stuck intae the bevvy, like—'

'I believe you, Davie, I believe you implicitly. Scottish machismo begins and ends with "bevvy", as some of us have discovered more than once.'

And she goes on needling the pair of them, never noticing that Hamish is looking really ill. All the colour has drained from his face and he looks quite distracted. Then all of a sudden he starts burbling a lot of nonsense about a big fluffy chow and how he put out his hand to pat it and it snapped at him. And Cynthia asks if this happened in the Reeperbahn, and Hamish says, *Oh no, it was somewhere in Morningside*, and it's obvious that he's way back in his childhood. At this point Cynthia gets suddenly all concerned.

'Hamish, darling, look at me – are you all right? Oh, God!'

'Then it opened its mouth,' whispers Hamish, trembling and wild-eyed, 'I caught a glimpse of its great red tongue. I could see almost right down its throat, its upper lip was curled away from its great white fangs . . . *AAAH!*' With a strangled cry he slumps forward, head on table.

'Oh, my God! No! Hamish! Hamish! Wake up, darling! Jim, Davie, do something!'

'Oh, dear, dear,' fusses Arbuthnot, 'he's unconscious! Is it the syndrome, do you think – are these the symptoms?'

'That's the way my auntie was took,' says Davie, 'the verra same.'

'Oh, Hamish, please don't die – not now! You mustn't die among Dutchmen!'

Arbuthnot can't find a pulse and the waiter rushes over. Pandemonium breaks loose, then the doctor arrives and Hamish is carried off on a stretcher, followed by the hysterical Cynthia, with Davie and the minister trailing after them.

'They say it's a completely painless death, Cynthia,' says Davie comfortingly.

All is gloom and despondency. An hour passes, and Davie and the minister have heard nothing. As he paces the deck, the Rev. Arbuthnot is already beginning to compose in his mind the little 'Act of Remembrance' which he plans for the following day, before the remains are removed from on board.

'I pray to God the end comes swiftly,' he tells Davie, sighing and shaking his head. 'I saw death in his face yesterday. Oh, poor Cynthia!'

'He tellt me to look eftir Cynthia when he was gone, Jim. When he felt death approaching.'

'Ah, indeed? It's a solemn charge, David. Do you feel equal to the task?'

'Ach, well. We'll dae wur best, ken.'

'I couldn't feel any pulse, you know, David, none at all. I knew then there was no hope.'

'The Grim Reaper, Jim. Comes tae us a'.'

And no sooner are these solemn words out of his mouth, than who should appear beside them on deck, pale but joyful, but Sir Hamish Cadfoot, accompanied by Cynthia and the ship's doctor!

'Raisin' o' Lazarus, eh Jim?' says Davie, never short of a quip.

And it transpires at once that there isn't a great deal wrong with Hamish after all, and if he looks after himself he could even live to a ripe old age.

'But – the syndrome?' asks the poor minister almost querulously, feeling the little Act of Remembrance slipping from his grasp for ever. 'Do you not have the syndrome after all?'

'Oh, I've got it all right, but it seems I picked up the wrong end of the stick from my specialist. You know how it is when you're depressed and expecting the worst! You see, he told me that my condition was "incurable", and I took that to mean, you know, "fatal" . . . silly, I know.'

'Well, Sir Hamish, postural-sacral redundancy syndrome never killed anyone!' the doctor assures him, smiling unctuously.

'Except Davie's auntie, so it seems!' Cynthia butts in with her usual heavy sarcasm.

'Did ye say *postural*-sacral redundancy syndrome, doctor? That's no whit ma auntie had, naw, naw . . . It was *posterior*-sacral redundancy syndrome, I'm shair o' that.'

'Ah, yes. Now that's a very different kettle of fish. You can die of that, all right. Quite distinct from Sir Hamish's condition.'

'Oh, Hamish,' chirrups Cynthia, 'what a preposterous, darling old fraud you are! But I love you.' And she kisses him on the cheek.

'Anyway,' says the doctor, 'this attack had nothing to do with the syndrome. It's the result of overwrought nerves compounded with excessive consumption of alcohol over a period of several days. Basically, he just fainted.'

So there it was. The next day Hamish and Cynthia went into Amsterdam by themselves to celebrate – 'our second honeymoon', as the lady called it – and Davie was left to explore the delights of that liberated metropolis in the sparkling company of the Rev. James Arbuthnot.

And two days later they're back at Leith Docks. Hamish and Cynthia are leaning on the rail, and Davie's hanging around shyly, waiting for the right moment to say farewell.

'Well, darling,' Hamish is saying, 'here we are. Home again . . . like waking from a living nightmare.'

'Oh no, Hamish, a dream, a beautiful dream! Who would have thought when we set off that I'd end up the Most Glamorous Granny and Queen of the Ship?'

Then they see their daughter waiting on the quay with little Samson, and a right pantomime ensues.

'Oh! Look, darling – he's waving!' coos Cynthia. 'Little Samson is waving! Bless his little heart! He's waving at his Glamorous Granny! Hooee! He-llo, Samson! Who loves his Granny?'

'Well, there we are then,' puts in Davie when the excitement's died down a bit. 'Home Sweet Home. The time has come, as they say.'

'Davie! We were just talking about you – worried we were going to miss you. Davie, it's been great sharing a table with you. It has so much enhanced our enjoyment of the whole trip. Put it there, pal!'

And the two pals shake hands.

'Cynthia – ma Queen for a night. What can ah say?'

'Say nothing, Davie. Farewell, sweet prince.' And she offers Davie her cheek to peck.

Then Sir Hamish clears his throat and begins to look a bit official.

'Well, Davie . . . Don't know when we'll be seeing you again.'

Davie doesn't know how to respond to that at all, but what he finds himself saying, willy-nilly, is:

'Ay, well, let's see, sir . . . Young Stuart plays pool on a Monday . . . It'll likely be either Tuesday or Wednesday of next week, sir. We'll get thae doors hung for ye, nae bother. If it's no Tuesday it'll be Wednesday, that's a promise!'

7

Aldengrave the Alchemist

Victor Aldengrave, though sometimes an aggressively prickly individual, was at bottom a withdrawn soul whose tendency was to shrink with distaste from the hugger-mugger of life-as-she-is-lived into the protective shell of abstruse learning and self-imposed eremitism. He would set out bravely on some challenging adventure, but soon lose his nerve and retreat into the known and familiar, in a recidivistic pattern which by the end of his youth had left him isolated and lonely. On leaving university, for instance, he had departed Scotland to teach in France, but immediately found himself unable to absorb so much new and strange experience fast enough to remain functional in his work, and was home again within a couple of months. Undeterred, he next decided to emigrate to America, obtained the necessary visa and work permit and even had a job lined up in Boston. But on arrival in New York City he felt so overwhelmed by the noise, the clamour, the multiplicity, and above all the overbearing pressure of the towering buildings on his vertiginous spirit, that he decided to take a holiday instead: he retreated to a small village in New England, stayed there for a fortnight and then came back home again.

After that he decided to train as a librarian – just as a fall-back position, for he still had an unaccountable urge to depart, to explore, to leave behind the comfortable and familiar and strike out for the latter ends of the earth. But this impulse was almost entirely fed by books; and as the years passed, Aldengrave became discomfitingly aware of his inability to see it through, to bring any of his multifarious dreams and schemes out of his head and into lived reality. Of course, this was not an inalterable condition, and he knew that too. He could have worked against his weakness, tested himself and advanced through small gains towards at least a partial mastery of his deep-rooted fear of life. But for reasons which he never allowed to become clear to himself, he did not do so.

So Aldengrave settled down in Edinburgh, where he eventually found himself in charge of a small branch library. His exploratory urge, self-frustrated, mutated from a spatial to a temporal orientation, and he buried himself in the past, which he could explore in a controlled way, at his own pace, by his own fireside, and was able to turn away from at any moment he felt like it; the past, which didn't importune him with unlooked-for challenges and overwhelming demands. So he obsessively followed the obscurest byways of medieval and Renaissance thought, and travelled mentally with those daring seekers who had lived on the outer edge of their times – inspired heresiarchs and crazy ascetics, magicians, alchemists and wandering scholars – whose pioneering adventures of the mind were often enough lived out in dramatic and romantic outward circumstances. And it was in such colourful company that Victor Aldengrave passed his time and lived vicariously – by himself in a small flat full of books.

His friends were all old friends whom circumstances had thrown in his way, and they were enough for him; he felt disinclined to take the risk involved in initiating and developing new relationships. He had had one romantic liaison, passionately obsessive, which had turned out badly, and thereafter decided that his own company was probably the best, and certainly the most to be trusted. But it must not be supposed that Aldengrave was outwardly of a shy and shrinking demeanour. In circumstances of his own choosing he could be sociable and even good company, though inclined, too, to be relentlessly scathing and abrasive about the vulgarities and idiocies of the modern world, from which he felt himself radically alienated.

His historical researches were not entirely without their fruits. He published, for instance, in a learned journal, a commendable study of the little-known medieval heretic Gaspare of Fiesole, a Franciscan disciple of Joachim of Fiore and elaborator of the latter's influential ideas on the coming Age of the Holy Spirit. In correspondence with another Joachite, Gerard of Borgo San Donnino, Gaspare appears, in a discussion of the Annunciation, to express the view that the Holy Spirit came to the Blessed Virgin in the form of a male apparition: 'when she beheld that form overshadow her, and felt those arms enfold her . . . ' (These words were only made public long after Gaspare's death, else he must surely have shared Joachim's condemnation by the Fourth Lateran Council in 1215.) By some historians of the period these remarks of Gaspare's had been considered merely an incautious use of metaphorical language, but Aldengrave argued convincingly for their literal intent, seeing them as adumbrating a kind of Docetism turned on its head. It was an impressive thesis which caused quite a stir in the relevant academic circles – rather restricted ones, it has to be said.

By the time he was forty, both Aldengrave's parents had died and he had inherited a little money. One Saturday afternoon he was making for the Pentland Hills to take a long walk when he got caught up in a traffic jam. The cars were moving sluggishly down the swiftly clogging bypass as the exit to the vast shopping complex drew near. Their occupants, he knew, were off to demonstrate their spending power, empowered to make lifestyle choices by the freedom afforded by two incomes. How very much better, Aldengrave suddenly thought, to be remotely ensconced in some mountain fastness, immersed in profound studies of the old alchemists, in the disinterested but perennially interesting pursuit of elusive Truth, simply sustained by the proceeds of a modest but sufficient portfolio earned by the industry and acumen of one's forebears, 'while branches and rain hurl themselves at the library windows,' cocking a snook at postmodernist relativism!

So he resigned from his post at the library and removed to a remote cottage in Moray, on the edge of a moor. He loved the impersonality of the moor, or rather he loved its personality which was not a human personality, but which became more intimate to him than any human person had ever been. For him there was no monotony in it, but a complex and ever-changing multiplicity which spoke to him in a language which he came to see was more inward than any which made use of words. He would have been happy enough to spend the rest of his days just wandering on the moor; so, at least, it sometimes seemed to him.

Yet he still loved words too. During his years on the moor he was working on a fictionalized account of the life of the Scottish alchemist Alexander Seton, known as 'the Cosmopolite', an 'intellectual nomad' who at the beginning of the seventeenth century cut a romantic swathe across Europe, performing spectacular transmutations of base metal into gold and eventually dying tragically as a result of his dedication to demonstrating the truth of the alchemical art.[1]

In his novelistic biography, Aldengrave told how in 1601 Seton succoured a Dutch sea captain, Jacob Hanssen, whose ship had been wrecked on the Scottish coast – he gave immediacy to this scene by setting it on the Moray Firth. He then described how Seton, visiting his Dutch friend at Enkhuysen the following year, converted a small amount of lead into an equal weight of gold, marking the alchemical product with the date and time (4 p.m. on 13 March 1602), and presented it to the captain. Eventually this alchemical gold passed to one Daniel Georg Morhof, a man of learning who told this part of the story in his *De Metallorum Transmutatione*, published in Hamburg in 1673.

---

[1] What follows summarizes the engaging account to be found in John Read, *Humour and Humanism in Chemistry* (London, 1947).

From Holland Seton progressed, accompanied by a red-headed Scottish retainer called William Hamilton, via Italy to Switzerland, encountering on his journey a sceptical academic named Johann Wolfgang Dienheim, a professor at Freiburg, who described him as of 'middle age, intelligent and very modest in his demeanour, and of a sanguine temperament'. The adept was small but robust, with a fresh complexion and neatly trimmed chestnut-brown beard, and wore a habit of figured black satin. When they reached the Golden Stork tavern at Basel, Seton undertook to cure Dienheim of his distrust of the Hermetic art by practical demonstration; and summoning as a further witness one Dr Jacob Zwinger, professor of Greek at Basel and also an authority on medicine, he performed at a local goldsmith's shop a spectacular transmutation, converting lead mixed with sulphur into the purest gold by the agency of a tiny amount of a heavy, greasy powder. His scepticism utterly overturned, Dienheim now came to regard the Scottish alchemist as: 'a great and sacred man – a demigod!'

Aldengrave in his turn was quite carried away by the figure of this long-ago Scot who had blazed a meteor trail across Europe for a few brief years and then perished in his pride. With inspired pen he brought to life the Cosmopolite's strange adventures in Strassburg, where he began to assume false identities; in Frankfurt am Main, where he posed as a French count; in Cologne, where he received from a fellow Scot called Master George a warning which fell on deaf ears; at Helmstedt, where he confuted a professor of philosophy; and at Munich, where he succumbed to the charms of a burgher's daughter, and to matrimony.

But now it fell to Aldengrave to depict the final, tragic scenes in the lurid story of the wandering Cosmopolite. In the autumn of 1603 Seton was in Crossen in Saxony, where the court of the Elector Christian II was in residence. There he delegated his red-headed servant to perform an alchemical demonstration which proved so successful that Seton and his wife were invited to accompany the court to Dresden. (William Hamilton had by this time shrewdly departed for home.) It soon became clear that the sadistic and avaricious young Elector was determined to extract the Cosmopolite's secret by fair means or foul. Failing with flattery and cajolery, the Neronic ruler consigned Seton to the torture chamber, where he was repeatedly racked and burned with red-hot irons. In Cologne the alchemist had told Master George that he would sooner die than give up his secret, and he proved as good as his word, remaining stubbornly silent through every agony, until the Elector, fearing that he would die with his secret still undisclosed, removed him to solitary confinement in a hateful dungeon.

There he languished for three months until a Polish or Moravian nobleman called Michael Sendivogius, or Sensophax, an enthusiast for alchemy who was living in Dresden at the time, managed to effect his rescue by carrying through a cunning and carefully prepared plan. Seton, broken by torture, was removed from the prison by Sendivogius in a carriage, in which – joined by the alchemist's wife with the tincture – they fled to Cracow, where he died in January 1604 as a result of his ordeal. His rescuer fell heir to his powder, his wife, and, it seems likely, his treatise *Novum Lumen Chymicum*, which under the name of Sendivogius – who was to enjoy an almost equally spectacular career before descending into charlatanry – maintained its popularity for generations to come.

Such was the romantic tale – though recounted soberly enough and with a great deal of circumstantial detail in the original sources – with which Aldengrave was obsessively exercised in his years by the moor in Moray. Identifying himself strangely with the old adept who, in his daring extraversion and fearless adventurousness, was so strikingly unlike him, he began to believe that the Cosmopolite's life story held some hidden meaning for himself. At least, that is how it appears from some of the multifarious notes and jottings he left behind at his untimely death. Immersed in the theory of alchemy, in person lean, wild-haired and stooping, he appeared increasingly eccentric to his scattered neighbours, who, making the best use of his sonorous surname (which, by the way, derives from the Berwickshire place-name *Auchencraw* – Aldengrave hated it when it was assumed to be English), inevitably christened him 'Aldengrave the Alchemist'.

It is far from clear what strange thoughts must have been jostling in Aldengrave's mind in the course of the year or two after the completion of his book on the Cosmopolite. It would appear that he had read Jung's classic *Psychology and Alchemy* and been influenced by its account of alchemy as a projection of a psychic process of transformation; but, if his fragmentary notes can be taken as a trustworthy indicator of his understanding and his state of mind, he seems to have been oddly obtuse about both Jung's meaning and any possible application to his own case. Aldengrave had always been of an obsessively introverted nature, and it appears likely that long-standing isolation, and total immersion in arcane material, had compromised his judgement and atrophied his powers of discrimination. It may not be overstating the case to raise the question of mental imbalance.

Briefly, he had come to share the conviction of the old alchemists that the human mind carries within it a kind of magical power capable of transforming even recalcitrant matter itself. If it could work thus on the inanimate world, was it not, *a fortiori*, inherently capable of altering its own constitution and character? For the philosopher's stone was man himself, and there existed an identity between man and something which lay concealed within matter. Aldengrave underlined a quotation from Gerhard Dorn's *Philosophia meditativa*: 'Thou wilt never make from others the One that thou seekest, except there first be made one thing of thyself'; that is to say, the alchemical adept must accomplish internally, in his own psyche, the same process which he seeks to induce in matter.

Aldengrave appears to have been struck by the conformity of Alexander Seton's character as described by Dienheim with the requirements for the successful adept outlined by Geber in the *Rosarium philosophorum*. He must be: 'firm in purpose, persevering, mild, long-suffering and good-tempered.' This contrasted in a number of ways with his own character; and irresolution and vacillation were serious disqualifications for the devotee of Hermetic art. Looking back at the failures and disappointments of his own life, Aldengrave seems to have determined to transform his psychic constitution by an obscure process which he came to believe was a contemporary equivalent of the alchemical enterprise. But he was fatally blind to Jung's crucial insight that the adept's projection of his own unknown psychic background into the darkness of matter was not intentional, but an involuntary occurrence.

It is here that Aldengrave's overwhelming sense of identity with the moor beside which he lived comes into play. Humanly isolated, the eccentric author felt himself more and more involved with the materiality of his surroundings; and the idea which came to obsess him was that if he could penetrate, by an act of mental empathy and entering-in, the inner nature of the material world, then that secret thing which lay hidden within it, which alchemical doctrine taught was identical with his own nature, would silently work upon him and transform his psychic constitution, drawing him away from the irremediable suffering of the world and opening up to him an unseen realm of wholeness and harmony.

This account of Aldengrave's purpose and state of mind is constructed from evidence which is suggestive but not conclusive, for his notes are disjointed and sometimes cryptic and written in a language which is to some extent private. What seems to have worked on his mind in his final months was at once an agonized, unappeased longing to sink his identity in his material environment, and a half-acknowledged recognition of the final irremediable elusiveness of such a goal. But who can hope to explain the roots of another's despair? Every person who despairs has arrived at his or her own despair, that is like no-one else's but fits the individual personality like a glove. And why can one struggle with infinite pains out of a slough of despond, while another only wallows helplessly and is sucked in deeper, and a third plunges wilfully down with a thrawn, morose determination?

A Scots poem Aldengrave wrote around this time can be read as either consciously or unconsciously prophetic; it is hard to decide whether it expresses an intention already present in its author's mind, or whether the writing of it somehow evoked, or laid bare, a purpose hitherto shadowy or uncertain:

> I am a man forsakit by the sun
> Shauchlin throu snaw-drifts tae the warld's end,
> An whatna airt I tak, it's aa the same—
> Daith meets me ony gate, an I neednae run.
> I cannae find, nor cannae tine the wey,
> Aathing is dwinin, an my day is dune;
> I cannae thole the mindin o thae een,
> I cannae thole the licht o the thrawn mune.
> Ettlin tae fill my life wi an endless darg
> I thocht tae mak a lowe loup in my breist:
> Increasin knowledge; lust in a pokie room;
> But dowf was my body an my saul aye toom.
> Nou I am trachled by the need tae speak,
> Farfochen i the confines o my saul;
> Gin I can win the howe o thon laigh gowl
> There I'll lie doun, as aye I hae, my lane.
> Alane, the lift abune; ablow, the snaw.
> I cannae understaun my deemless pain.
> Nae greetin. Sleep cancels aa.
> It's gane.

One day in the late February of his fifty-first year Victor Aldengrave drove to a spot on the moor road not far from

Lochindorb, seven or eight miles south of his cottage, and abandoning his car, walked off into the open country. He headed west across the moorland, then, it appears – for he seems to have been sighted once – turned south and followed for a time the rough track by the Leonach Burn. Just at that time fierce blizzards swept across the country on a north-westerly gale. And it must have been in these atrocious conditions that Aldengrave pressed on alone, following the course of Allt a Choire Odhair Mhoir, up between Carn Glas and Carn Allt Laoigh.

This time, for once, he did not turn back.

8

Plaintiff

Sad as an empty haggis skin, I was out for a walk one day with my wife's little dog, Plaintiff (strange name for a dog, you're thinking: I agree), when he got stuck down a rabbit hole. At least I assumed at the time that he had got stuck, because he went in and never came out again.

'Oh dear,' I thought, because Madeleine was very fond of Plaintiff, though I can't myself imagine why.

At this juncture a very small man with pointed ears appeared from nowhere and said:

'If you want to see Plaintiff ever again you'd better come with me.'

I didn't, as a matter of fact, have the slightest desire to see Plaintiff ever again, but I was thinking of Madeleine, so I decided I'd better go.

'Before you go down there,' he said, pointing to the rabbit hole, 'I'm going to have to give you something to make you small.' At one time I would have assumed that the little man was a fairy, but no-one with any sense believes in fairies any more, so I suppose he must have been an alien.

As soon as I had swallowed – without water, which was rather unpleasant – the surprisingly large pill which the little man gave me, I also became very small, and green, like him. I can't say whether my ears became pointed because I didn't have a mirror with me. But I certainly did become extremely small, and oddly enough so did my clothes; which is just as well, for otherwise I would undoubtedly have been overwhelmed and perhaps smothered by my enveloping garments.

I followed the odd little person underground.

As we trudged down the steeply descending, sandy-bottomed burrow he remarked to me over his shoulder:

'It isn't by chance, you know, that your dog has come down here. He has come down for a definite purpose, and one that has to do with you.'

'He isn't my dog,' I replied a trifle testily. 'He's my wife's.'

The alien, if that's what he was, merely shrugged his shoulders and gave a little snort, as if he felt I was being pedantic. But accuracy has always been important to me, and besides I didn't want to be identified as the owner of such a creature as Plaintiff. And although I was curious to know what Plaintiff's purpose in entering the burrow might have been, and how it might concern myself, I didn't wish to appear over-eager and so decided to keep my mouth shut.

I had never been down a rabbit hole before, so everything was new to me. The first surprising thing was that there was no sign of any rabbits. Spiders, on the other hand, there were in plenty. The entire filthy, dusty network of corridors through which we were making our confusing way was infested by huge and revolting arachnids which scampered around in a threatening manner and dangled menacingly from the ceiling.

'This, by the way, is the realm of Unplease,' my guide informed me. I was not surprised. 'Here, everything is very difficult, and truth hard to discern.'

I didn't reply, and the alien, evidently piqued, continued his observations in a slightly hectoring tone, or so it seemed to me.

'All this is being done for your own good, you know,' he said. 'You have been depressed recently, and I shrewdly suspect that you are holding down a great deal of repressed anger. Plaintiff has been sent down here expressly at my behest, to take you on a little journey which I hope will be of benefit to you. But I'm not looking for thanks.'

None of this made the slightest sense to me, need I say.

'I've come with you to retrieve the dog, and for no other reason,' I said stiffly.

'*Tick, tick, tinn,*' remarked my guide, gazing up at the ceiling as he walked.

'I beg your pardon?'

'*Tick, tick, tinn,*' stubbornly repeated the asinine little fellow, and relapsed into silence.

I was getting fed up with this, and, shouldering my way past my *soi-disant* benefactor, I began to stride out in the hope of catching up with the wretched Plaintiff and making my way back above ground, out of the realm of Unplease and into that of sanity. But as I rounded a bend a fist-sized, hairy spider dropped from the ceiling on to my shoulder and bit me on the ear. I let out a cry of outrage and disgust and the beast dropped to the floor: I took off my shoe and tried to kill it, but immediately several others came whizzing around my head, brushing my scalp and dropping great wads of dust and brownish powder all over me. I was struggling ineffectually with these monsters when the little man caught up with me and in an authoritative tone called them off with the words, '*Tinn, tinn, tick!*' Instantly they all scuttled off.

'That was very foolish,' said my guide. 'You have not up till now come to severe harm down here – solely because you are under my protection. You have many natural enemies in the realm of Unplease. One does not come down here and emerge unchanged, but if you do as you're told the changes can be for the better. If you don't, they will undoubtedly be for the worse.'

Chastened, I merely nodded my head. A large throbbing inflammation was already distorting my ear, and various other parts of my body where the spiders had bitten me had begun to itch and smart. I decided not to argue.

A little way on and a young girl in rags emerged from a squalid chamber leading off the corridor we were pursuing. She was carrying what appeared to be a baby, but nothing of it was visible, the whole being wrapped from top to bottom and completely enveloped in a profusion of filthy shawls.

'Have pity, sir,' the girl said, stepping forward shyly yet boldly and placing a hand on my forearm. 'Oh, have pity!'

'The baby – it's mine, isn't it?' I asked, gripped at once by an obscure conviction of identity. 'Why do you have it all wrapped up in that way – surely it's going to suffocate?'

The girl half shook her head. Not, I felt, in denial, but rather as if I could not be expected to understand. Her lips moved once more in silent pleading. In my perplexity I turned towards my diminutive mentor for guidance.

'The child will not suffocate,' the odious little know-all announced, 'for a very good reason. It has not yet grown a head. That is why it has to be kept covered up.'

He smiled smugly and, taking my arm, pulled me away from the girl, who stretched out a forlorn hand to detain us as we moved on. I gestured back at her despairingly. What could I have done anyway? How could I help a baby to grow a head? But all the same I muttered a brief prayer to St Tordealbhach, associated in the Celtic tradition with generation.

I stumbled wearily on, my guide keeping up a brisk pace through the debris-ridden tunnels we were traversing. I presumed we were still supposed to be pursuing Plaintiff, but I couldn't imagine how the little man could guess his route amid the confusion of channels in this hideously complex warren. Soon I heard horrendous screams issuing from a kind of cavern to our left.

'Down here you will find both good things and bad things,' said the little alien, noticing my concern. 'In there, for instance, they are torturing a postmodernist.'

'Is that a good thing or a bad thing?' I asked.

'That depends entirely on your point of view,' he replied. 'Everything is relative.'

I should have guessed. 'But how did he come to be here?'

'Horribly shipwrecked on a sea awash with floating signifiers, he fell into our hands. Now they are conducting an experiment. At present, you see, he maintains that there is no reality but language. They wish to establish whether he will ever come to the opinion that pain, too, is a reality.' And indeed I could hear the hapless theorist being subjected in the torture chamber to a fiendish interrogation.

'He is bound to an Ixionic wheel,' the alien expanded helpfully. 'That is the nature of his torment.'

'We want the truth!' shouted one of his tormentors. 'We have meaningful ways of making you talk!'

'The truth! How can I tell you the truth when I don't know what that means? Don't you see – there is no such thing as truth!'

'We want the truth! And we have all the time in the world . . . '

'But I can't tell you the truth, can I, when there are so many truths! . . . Oh, have mercy!'

'The truth, the whole truth and nothing but the truth! Bind him tighter, Ludwig!'

'Aaaah! *Whose* truth? Whose truth do you *want*? I'm willing to give you *anyone*'s truth . . . '

'*Anyone*'s truth? A minute ago you were saying there was no such thing as truth! Look, this is the real world, pal! Bind him tighter, Ludwig! – Now, let's be having the truth, pal!' yelled the demonic essentialist.

'No, no! Don't ask me for the truth – anything but that!'

And so it would go on, through all eternity.

Soon after this I caught just a glisk of Plaintiff's tail disappearing round a bend. The alien increased his pace. On all sides there were casual horrors – maimed, indifferent beggars, crudely amputated limbs, piles of bloody excrement. Amorphous slug-like creatures infested the weeping walls of the caves. In a niche, suspended from a meat-hook by a kind of dreadlock, I saw a severed head. With shock too profound to describe I recognized it as my own. The eyes were closed and the head appeared lifeless; but as I watched with fascinated repulsion the eyelids opened and blinked, the lips twitched and other signs of animation followed. A little colour seeped into the livid cheeks. I gazed at the head and the head gazed back at me in sickened communion.

But the little alien seemed pleased. He smiled at me complacently as if to say, 'What did I tell you?' and pulled me away from the spot. And his evident optimism appeared not unfounded, for we soon emerged unexpectedly from the foul region in which we had been sojourning and stood before the entrance to a pale, empty, domed chamber. There was no-one in it and the curved whitish walls were devoid of ornament. Complete silence reigned here. Over the door was a plain plaque with an inscription:

The poet or seer creates within himself a space or void within which he can meet the absent God.

The little man requested me to sit down on the floor.

'I am going to leave you now,' he said. 'In due course a new guide will come to take charge of you. This may take some time, but don't worry. The time will pass quickly.'

'But what about the dog?' I asked fretfully. 'You told me that it was the dog who was taking me on this little journey. I saw his tail disappearing round a corner a little while ago – if I wait here I'll certainly lose him again.'

'Don't worry about the dog. His turn comes later. Everything has to work itself out according to a predetermined pattern, you see. Just wait here and don't worry.'

I was far from satisfied with any of this but there was little I could do. The alien left me and I sat on for a long time in this place of utter silence and complete abstraction. At least I have to assume that it was a long time, but there was nothing to measure time by and at the end of it, as the little man had indicated, it had not seemed long to me. At first I thought a little about the inscription above the door. Although I have never had any aspirations to be either a poet or a seer, nevertheless, I thought (for I come from Edinburgh), its message seemed to carry a burden of expectation which I was not confident I could measure up to. The fact was that I had no idea how to create a space or void within myself. So I just sat there patiently, and nothing much seemed to happen, either within me or without. Possibly, after all, nothing was supposed to happen.

Then a woman appeared from the door opposite on a bicycle. A startlingly attractive woman, actually, admittedly not in the first flush of youth but nonetheless younger than me and well preserved, as they say. It was a pity she was dressed in a jogging top and stretch nylon ski pants, but I was not in a position to be choosy. I noticed she had several valuable-looking rings on her fingers. I thought her a bit *nouveau-riche*, to be honest, as opposed to myself who am decidedly *nouveau-pauvre*. But as the poet asserted:

> We *nouveaux pauvres* are always proud:
> We stand up straight, with heads unbowed.
> We may be poor, but we can teach
> A few things to the *nouveaux riches*.

However that may be, the lady was friendly.

'You must come with me,' she said, smiling encouragement. 'I have been detailed to conduct you on the next stage of your journey. I am the Lady of the Château McGlumpha, by the way,' she added holding out her hand.

But, goodness me, when I tried to respond, I found I had forgotten my own name! It was incredibly embarrassing. I stumbled and stuttered and tried to pretend I had been going to say something else, but I couldn't for the life of me think of anything I might plausibly have been going to say. And indeed, the whole time I remained with the McGlumpha lady – a long time as it turned out – I never did succeed in remembering my name. I put it down to stress. I had been through some nasty experiences during the last however-long-it-was, not least with the spiders. I was now covered with large, suppurating red blotches, by the way, and was a most unsightly sight. But since the alien left me I was at least no longer green. As to my size I don't know, for everyone was on the same scale in this part of the world and the question was no longer meaningful.

'Well, Tom,' the lady said (no doubt to cover my embarrassment – although I couldn't remember my name I was quite sure that it wasn't Tom), 'we're going to have to do something about those bites. The fact is, I fancy you something rotten, but at the moment you scarcely look your best.' And she gave me some salve which cured them instantly and restored me to my usual fanciable self.

I won't go into everything that followed. We had a rough passage in places, she seated perjink on the bicycle and I riding pillion and hanging on to her breasts for dear life, but she steered us confidently through all the glaur and slurry and worse which we encountered on the country roads (we had left the underground realm of Unplease behind when we emerged from the domed chamber). The thing was that I was in love and impervious to external woes, and also unfazed by all the bizarre things she said to me as we continued on our way. To give an example:

'You have always believed, haven't you,' she remarked, 'that your paternal grandfather died of a heart attack after attempting to separate two fighting dogs? That's the story they told you?'

'Well, yes, as a matter of fact it is—'

'I'm afraid it's not true. In reality he was killed while watching a bullfight in Spain. The bull broke through the barrier and your grandfather, sitting in the front row, was blinded in one eye and badly wounded. He died of shock.'

Naturally I was surprised. But that was only one of many things she put me right about in the days, months and perhaps years that followed.

'You have been living on illusions all your life,' the lady said to me one day. 'It's time for all that to stop. When you leave me you'll realize what's what, and consequently others will be able to rely on what you tell them. When that's not the case . . . nothing can work properly, you know.'

After various trials and tribulations we arrived at the Château McGlumpha. It proved to be a rather luxurious caravan on a site near a seaside town which from a distance seemed to me suspiciously like Burntisland; but the lady assured me that we were far distant from Middle Earth. Perhaps we were in a parallel universe containing an exact replica of Burntisland. Anyway, I stayed there with her for quite some time. Her man was not around: he worked far away in the oil industry, or so she told me. She had advised me to keep my mouth shut and not speak to anyone on the site, and to encourage the notion that I was dumb I sometimes spoke to the lady in sign language. But I don't want to say much more about any of this, for after all I am a married man and I don't want to hurt Madeleine, even though it all happened in another country, and for all I know the wench involved may be dead.

One day after I had been enjoying the lady's company for what felt to me like only a few days, though she claimed that it had been a great deal longer, she said to me:

'It's time you were on your way, Tom. No, please don't argue. The fact is that I'm expecting an important visitor tonight and if he finds you here you'll be in deep trouble. Besides which, you have a further journey to make yourself. Your stay here has equipped you for that, in that you're now a completely reliable person, which I have to say you weren't before. I'm going to take you back to the dome now, and you'll see your little friend there. But he in his turn will hand you over to your faithful dog Plaintiff, who has been waiting patiently for you all these years.'

'Could you not take me on the rest of my journey yourself?' I pleaded. 'I much prefer your company to Plaintiff's.'

'You can be guided there only by an innocent being who loves you unreservedly. I do love you, but not without reservations. And I am, as you know, far from innocent.'

'Is that it, then? Am I never to see you again?'

'Hmm . . . Keep a look-out for me and someday you might be lucky.'

We journeyed back to the dome on the most delightful of May days. Songbirds chorused joyfully, rabbits and roe deer disported themselves in the water meadows, butterflies fluttered around our heads in a riot of lightness and colour. As the poet sang:

> Cabbage white, O cabbage white!
> I praise your soaring, beauteous flight.
> With one flap of each tiny wing
> You change the climate in Peking.

The lady and I drifted along in silent regret at our coming separation. As we approached the little beech grove from which, in the entrails of an ancient gnarled tree, the passageway emerged which led to the domed chamber, the girl whom I had seen earlier, carrying the headless baby, came out to greet us. She still bore the infant, but now held it out in proud delight for us to admire: a fine, chuckling baby boy with a fully developed head. Tears glistened in her eyes.

'Thank you, sir . . . oh, thank you!' she whispered, and even tried to go down on her knees before me, which I found deeply embarrassing and forbade with a compassionate gesture. I had no idea what she was thanking me for but did not wish to seem ungraciously ungrateful for her gratitude, so I merely nodded, smiled, and muttered a few words to the effect that it had been a pleasure to be of assistance. She gave a kind of little curtsey and withdrew, and the lady and I passed on into the tunnel.

Walking slowly a little ahead of us I saw a small slightly bowed figure in a green tweed jacket, frail but yet giving an impression of an underlying sturdiness, his head surmounted by a deep, stiff brush of grey hair. I recognized him at once as the poet Hugh MacDiarmid (C.M. Grieve). He entered the domed chamber and made his way to a grand piano in the middle of the room, which had not been there on my previous visit. He jumped on to the piano stool with unexpected sprightliness, and without any pause began to play with astonishing virtuosity and passion. Although the music was familiar to me I could not identify it at the time, but I have since come to think that it must have been Beethoven's 'Apassionata' sonata. Musical performance had never, so far as I was aware, been one of the poet's accomplishments, but now, as if discovering his true essence for the first time, he was filling the domed room with all the consummate artistry of his soul. I was swept away by the music into a tremendous world of the spirit in which time and space meant nothing and here and now were contained only in the soaring sound which, I came on an instant to realize, was no sound at all, for it existed . . . only inside my own head. What exactly do I mean by that? I know, but I am unable to find the words. But the music I will never forget. Music that spoke of the flawed impassioned perfection of this mortal world and its glorious *felix culpa*. Whoever heard its like on earth or in story? Alas, it was that I heard it that destroyed me.

I closed my eyes as the music resounded, and when I opened them again at its close MacDiarmid was no longer there, nor was the Lady of the Château McGlumpha anywhere to be seen. Instead, the officious little green alien was standing at my elbow, smiling at me with insufferable self-satisfaction.

'You have now', he said in his tour-conductor's manner, 'come to the departure point of the last and most difficult part of your journey. In a very few minutes your wife's little dog Plaintiff will re-appear, to conduct you through a worm-hole into quite another part of the universe. It is inconceivably far away and has an infinite number of dimensions, but can be reached very quickly by means of this worm-hole, which doesn't yet exist but will come into existence through your use of it. There, the atoms of your body will be simultaneously enfolded into the entire structure of that which is, and you will exist everywhere and at all times.'

'Goodness!' I said. Such are the wonders of cosmology.

'In practice,' the little man went on, 'what you will experience is a world in which war, poverty, hunger, disease, infirmity, suffering, and above all death, do not exist. There is nothing there but order and beauty, richness, pleasure and peace. It is a world in which conflict, disharmony, child abuse, global warming and the slow withering of beauty are unknown, and everything is suffused by love. Also, everybody there speaks English. And here, if I am not mistaken, comes Plaintiff himself to lead you thither.'

And indeed, Plaintiff appeared on cue and came lolloping towards me joyfully, ears flapping and tail wagging in affectionate greeting. But some imp of the perverse made me reject his advances.

'I don't want to see this animal ever again,' I said.

'Fair enough, up to yourself,' said the little man, and instantly everything disappeared.

And I found myself once more alone on the bare hillside, and no sign of Plaintiff.

9

Monkey Tricks

The first school I attended was run by a pair of middle-aged women called Miss Faux (pronounced 'Fox') and Miss Todd. It was a nursery school, or 'kindergarten', to use the term then current, and occupied a three-storey terraced house at the end of a quiet cul-de-sac in a quiet suburb, above a grassy bank overlooking a tennis court. Behind the building was a pleasant garden which, however, because it was so heavily overspread by foliage for much of the year, seemed to me on gloomy or haary days to be an unfriendly and even sinister place. On the top floor of the house lived Miss Faux and Miss Todd, as well as Miss Faux's aged and rarely seen mother, from whom she had inherited the school, and who terrified me. I met her once in a shadowy corridor on my way to the bathroom, and with her stooped figure, angular features and black garments partly concealed by a voluminous grey woollen shawl, she seemed to me the very epitome of a witch. But the worst thing was that on her shoulder there perched a tiny monkey in a collar, with an old-seeming, knowing, wizened face and a searching gaze from its all-but-human eyes. After that I often had lurid nightmares about old Mrs Faux and her haunting familiar.

Miss Faux was an unlovely woman with greying, dandruff-ridden hair, who always wore an ill-fitting, sludge-green tailored suit which smelled musky and fousty. I thought her very old, but she was probably about forty-five. Miss Todd was similar in general style, but rather shorter and dumpier. She took the infants' class, while Miss Faux was responsible, with the help of a 'visiting' teacher, for the two higher classes. Miss Faux was sharper and more exacting than Miss Todd, and habitually addressed us children as 'You little monkeys!' On occasion, too, she could lose her temper rather impressively.

One afternoon, in the May of the last of my three years at the school, Miss Faux and Miss Todd held a tea party in the garden for the pupils. It must have been to celebrate something, but I have no recollection as to what. It was a beautiful early summer's day and the tables arrayed on the lawn with their white tablecloths were laden with goodies. Everyone, I felt, was ridiculously excited, but I was immune to the general mood. I was looking forward to the cakes, no doubt, but that was as far as it went; from all other points of view I would much rather have been at home. When we had played a few silly children's games, which I did my best to avoid, though not altogether successfully, Miss Todd clapped her hands to make an announcement.

'Today, boys and girls,' she proclaimed, 'we have a special surprise for you!' – and she extended her hand towards Miss Faux, who at that moment emerged from the back door with the monkey on her arm.

All the children whooped with delight, of course, but I backed away cautiously. My feelings about this animal were not such as to make his appearance a special treat for me. The existence of the monkey, whose name was Jacko – what else? – was generally known among the pupils, but I was one of the few who had actually laid eyes on him, which I think would have given me some degree of status had I let on. But I had kept this dark knowledge strictly to myself. This monkey, for me, was something much more than a mere object of vulgar curiosity, though I couldn't have put into words exactly what my feelings on the subject were.

In the balmy sunshine of the friendly afternoon Jacko was not, perhaps, quite the sinister personality of my first encounter. But I didn't see him as the others did. Miss Todd and Miss Faux were intent upon propagating an idea of the monkey as a 'naughty' creature, one whose antics could be guaranteed to provide an occasion for mirth and giggling. Jacko himself was living up to his role, a seemingly willing participant in what appeared to me something like a conspiracy. To my annoyance he pranced about the table while we were eating, and was really encouraged – in spite of the pretence of shock and outrage affected by the two mistresses – to eat somebody's ice cream, steal another's banana, grab a third's paper hat, or pull a girl's plaited pigtail.

'Oh, Jacko, what a wicked little monkey you are!' Miss Faux would screech, and all the children, but especially the girls, would put their hands to their mouths and giggle hysterically, and shout and jump up and down, and the boys would try to pull his tail, of course exciting the monkey even more and inciting him to further acts of engaging lawlessness. I felt obscurely angry on the animal's behalf because I knew he was being demeaned. But, since I could not articulate this sense to myself, what I experienced was only a vague alienation and animosity. I felt, now, that this creature whom I had so much feared, who had dogged and haunted my restless nights, had a secret connection with myself which placed me apart from all the others.

Perhaps Jacko himself felt, after a certain time, a disgust rising in his gorge at the way he was being used. Perhaps he said to himself, 'Enough's enough.' Or perhaps he just felt like exhibiting another side of what it is to be a monkey. Whatever the reason, after looking around a bit at his admiring audience and baring his teeth in the jackanapes manner, and scratching himself perfunctorily for fleas, he squatted down on his hunkers right in the middle of the centre table and there, amidst the sandwich fingers, the cream cookies, the éclairs and the Brunswick cake, he started to masturbate. The laughter trickled slowly away and a puzzled, uncertain silence settled upon all. But it was only brief. Before anyone had a chance even to enquire diffidently, 'What's the monkey doing?', Miss Todd exclaimed, 'Oh! – oh! – *oh!*' in a tone of flummoxed, flabbergasted outrage, and, snatching the startled and protesting animal up in mid-toss, dashed off with him towards the house, her heels splaying away from her left and right and the monkey chattering and squealing his strident vexation. But Miss Faux just stared at the ground with an abstracted, preoccupied kind of look, and repeated 'What a naughty monkey!' quite quietly, and almost, in fact, as if for her own benefit and instruction.

At the beginning of the following week Miss Faux had a new ploy for us. She wanted everyone to draw a picture of the monkey doing something naughty. It didn't matter what it was, it could be something the monkey had actually done at the tea party or something that came out of our own imaginations, just so long as it was something naughty. Each day she would come into the classroom and enquire archly:

'So what has that wicked monkey been up to today?'

And some days, since she was a *licenciée ès lettres*, she would ask the question in French:

'*Le singe malin, qu'est-ce qu'il fait ce matin?*' or:

'*Ce singe vilain, qu'est-ce qu'il fait aujourd'hui?*'

And over the course of the next few days everybody succeeded in producing some sort of approximation of a picture of Jacko up to his wicked tricks. Someone represented him stealing a banana, someone else depicted him eating somebody's ice cream, a third drew him grabbing hold of a paper hat and a fourth showed him tying a girl's pigtails together. Very few chose incidents which they had not witnessed, and many, inevitably, attempted the same scenes, so that there was quite a superfluity of treatments of Jacko's rather limited range of antisocial activities. But none of that appeared to matter to Miss Faux, since all of the drawings conformed to her instruction to show the monkey doing something *naughty* – all, that is, except mine.

For I was in the grip of an unaccountable imp of the perverse. This imp made me absolutely determined to portray the monkey doing nothing naughty, but on the contrary something as dignified or virtuous as possible. And I acted like this not at all because I was a virtuous little boy, but because I was the person I was and indeed still am to this day, and because I instinctively despised the received wisdom which teaches that monkeys do only naughty things.

So I drew the monkey preaching a sermon. When it had been explained to Miss Faux what the monkey was doing in my drawing, she was furious and told me that preaching a sermon was not naughty and that what I had been instructed to do was to draw the monkey doing something naughty. I was to go away and think about it and then come back with something that conformed to her stipulation. The following day I came back with a drawing of the monkey conducting a symphony orchestra – with the same result. Miss Faux was again furious and insisted that I would go on drawing pictures of the monkey until I had produced one that satisfied her requirements.

'That monkey does lots of wicked things which not a soul has drawn him doing yet!' And she gazed at me with a strange, wild, suggestive look in her eye.

I then produced a drawing of Jacko delivering a Report to an Academy, which elicited the response that I was a wicked boy.

Every morning at that time I woke early and lay in my bed thinking up new possibilities of portraying the monkey engaged in virtuous and dignified activities. But my imaginative resources were being taxed too heavily and I was running out of subjects. Then one day I heard my father reminiscing about how the streets of Edinburgh in his youth had been positively hotching with Italian organ grinders, all of them with their monkeys. Although I didn't really know what an organ grinder was, his remarks gave me the idea of a dramatic depiction of the monkey playing the great organ at our church. And I produced what was really a most impressive composition, with a fine sense of movement, showing the monkey with both hands raised over the two keyboards, his neck craning forward, his feet pumping away at the pedals, sweat dripping from his brow.

'You *wicked* boy!' Miss Faux exclaimed when she saw the drawing. 'You're mocking me! You know very well what I want you to do!'

And indeed I knew very precisely what was required of me. But I just stared at Miss Faux stony-faced.

'Jackanapes!' the teacher positively yelled. 'I've told you repeatedly that I want you to draw the monkey doing something *naughty*. Do I have to spell it out? Very well, then, I will. I want you to draw the monkey . . . playing with himself!'

Having said this at last, Miss Faux gasped and blanched and passed her hand over her forehead, and her mouth hung stupidly open. But I continued to stare at her stonily, and I know that my eyes now had the not-quite-human look of the eyes of the monkey himself.

Then Miss Faux stamped her foot and tore her hair and wept, but all to no avail. And the commotion brought Miss Todd through from the infants' class next door, and Miss Todd attempted to pacify her friend. But Miss Faux would not be comforted. And that same afternoon she was removed to a lunatic asylum on a hill, among trees, on the other side of town, and none of us ever saw her again. The monkey, I believe, was put down, and sole charge of the school was placed in the capable hands of Miss Todd.

Several parents withdrew their children, nonetheless.

10

Tom na Croiche

From the Papers of Robert Ballingall

Readers of this reminiscence may remember that strange business I got myself involved in years ago, over the death of the writer Leonard Balmain. He had appointed me his literary executor, and not long before his tragic end he had sent me, in that capacity, the manuscript on which he'd been working as a ghostwriter, the fictionalized biography of a person calling himself Torquil Tod, together with his own introductory memoir in which he repeatedly expressed the obsessive – but, I felt, well grounded – fear that his life was in danger from this Tod because of the grim story the latter had revealed to him. That story was one of a ritual cannibalistic infanticide committed by Torquil Tod and the child's mother, his partner in love and crime.[1]

---

[1] See the present writer's *Ghostwriting* (1996).

When, however, Balmain did die in violent but unexplained circumstances – his body discovered one Saturday night multiply broken at the foot of the stair well in the tenement block where he lived – there was no decisive evidence of foul play. A fall resulting from an attack of dizziness caused by Leonard's Menière's Disease was the generally accepted explanation, in spite of factors which in my view made this highly unlikely; but untold damage was done by a clever literary friend of the writer's, who touted the idea that Balmain's death was the suicide of a disappointed man in despair, who in a final act of postmodernist irony had stage-managed his own demise in a bizarre acting-out of 'The Death of the Author'. On this view 'Torquil Tod' never existed, but was an alter ego of the author's, a literary figure of his imagining whose function was symbolically to destroy him, and at the same time a shameless projection of his personal problems and obsessions.

I was greatly angered by this pretentious rubbish, and equally so by the disparaging obituary of Leonard which this so-called friend insulted his memory by perpetrating in a self-styled national newspaper. I therefore determined to make Balmain's history of 'Torquil Tod', together with his introductory memoir, available to the public, in the hope that some reader might be able to shed light upon the true identity of this murderous villain – light which could lead to his being brought to justice.

Just after I had penned my explanatory afterword, a missing continuation of Leonard's memoir, dealing with his relations with Tod after the completion of the biography, reached me anonymously through the post. I could not conceive who but Tod could have sent it.

Balmain had referred to this document in his letter to me, saying that he would forward it when it was completed. It never was, and no trace of either this or the original scripts of what he did send me were to be found among his papers at his death – a circumstance which convinced me of the truth of what he had written, and that these incriminating texts had been removed from the premises by his murderer. I decided to print this new evidence, the content of which confirmed with almost miraculous exactness everything which I had feared, along with the other texts, and without comment on the strange manner of its appearance, my silence an eloquent testimony to the correctness of my insights; but nothing whatever resulted. I suspect that most of the book's few readers found the whole business too complex and confusing.

In the years which followed I made every possible attempt to identify this Torquil Tod, with a view to tracking him down, but to absolutely no avail. He was clearly, by Balmain's account, a fiendishly clever man, and he had covered his tracks very effectively. Several times I imagined I was on the verge of a breakthrough, but every time the enticing threads vanished or dissolved or led into a cul-de-sac. I suppose it was because I was a very old friend of Leonard's, from university days, that I was so obsessive about avenging him. He was rather a pathetic person in some respects, but I was always fond of him, and loyalty is important to me. Besides which, I don't like it when people get away with things. I felt that Tod was secretly mocking me, and I kept him always at the back of my mind, hoping against hope that chance would one day provide me with the lead which, in spite of my diligence, his cunning had denied me.

Then, one morning a couple of years ago, I picked up in my doctor's waiting room a copy of a magazine called *Scottish Memories*, dated November 2000. There I happened upon a feature entitled 'The Beast's Legacy', by George Forbes, which I read with utter astonishment; for it recalled a real case which bore in all its essentials and in a striking number of particulars a quite extraordinary resemblance to the story of Torquil Tod and his woman Abigail as related to Leonard Balmain. The crucial events in this story took place exactly two years after the date assigned to the events narrated by Balmain; and at first, shaken by the apparent coincidence into doubting for the first time my own conviction that Leonard's tale of Torquil Tod was a straightforward account of the truth, I asked myself whether he might either have consciously based his work on his reading of newspaper accounts of this incident, or unconsciously have reproduced some of its elements from a submerged memory.

But a rapid reflection on the dates involved immediately reassured me on this point. In fact, Leonard Balmain had been fashioning his narrative out of Torquil Tod's recollections at the very time when the events recalled by George Forbes were being enacted! Moreover, these did not become news until two years after that date. So, if the relation between the two stories was anything more than that of coincidence (which I confess began to appear to me to be likely), subtler and more interesting explanations must be sought. For instance: most straightforwardly, could Torquil and Abigail's crime have been known about in occult circles, and imitated by the other couple? Or did both conform to some recurring or archetypal pattern influencing such events? Or again, and perhaps most intriguing, was it conceivable that Balmain, composing some elaborate, self-referential creative plan within his mind, somehow – given the seemingly preternatural receptiveness possessed by some artists – received within it telepathically the imprint of the savage events even then taking place, and unknowingly made them his own, but modified by the action of the conscious mind?

In order to give you a better handle on all of this, I shall now compare the two stories schematically, noting both their resemblances and their mutual deviations. For convenience I shall refer to the narrative written by Balmain as 'B', and the account penned by Forbes (which, remember, recounts publicly verifiable fact) as 'F'.

In B we find a girl from Dundee calling herself Abigail (really Annie), who has been to art college, become involved in occultism and the Black Arts, and drifts to London. In F we have a girl from Glasgow called Sheena who has been to college in Edinburgh, become involved in occultism and the Black Arts, and drifts to London. Both girls have been influenced by Aleister Crowley.

In B, Abigail when she goes to London is pregnant by a charlatan healer; there she meets a man called Torquil and they return together to their native Scotland. In F, Sheena becomes pregnant in a supposedly divine conception during magical ceremonies near Stonehenge; she returns to Glasgow and, about the time of her daughter's birth, becomes involved with a man named Alan.

Both Torquil and Alan are represented as being dominated by the psychic powers of their respective partners.

Both couples live in communes at points in their stories: Torquil and Abigail in Edinburgh and then in the

West Highlands, Sheena and Alan in North Uist. But in B this is before the infanticide takes place, in F after.

In B, Abigail's baby daughter is born in June and ritually sacrificed on 1 August, the feast of Lughnasadh, in a remote cottage in the Highlands. In F, Sheena's baby daughter, named Kether Boleskine, is born in May and ritually sacrificed towards the end of August near the banks of a Highland loch. Both couples part soon after the respective infanticides. In B, Abigail disappears and Torquil suffers a mental breakdown, eventually confessing to his part in the murder through the vehicle of his verbal narrative to Balmain. In F, Alan makes off, Sheena confesses to a new boyfriend, then suffers a mental breakdown and confesses to her mother. Both culprits in F are eventually brought to trial, Alan being sentenced to life imprisonment and Sheena getting off with five years as a result of her mental condition. The baby's body is never found. 'Detectives remain convinced', Forbes concludes, 'that there was some dark element of ritualistic sacrifice involved in Kether's murder, but the bizarre reasons behind it remain locked in the murky minds of the perpetrators.'

You will perhaps agree with me that the resemblances between the two stories are remarkable, especially considering how closely they coincide in time. And you may understand how I found the possible relation they bore to each other as intriguing and teasing as it was elusive. In fact I became obsessed with the project of discovering such a relation.

All this preyed on my mind until I felt compelled to make a trip into the Highlands to see for myself some of the places associated with the events recounted in the

Scottish Memories narrative. Though the identity of these places is quite within the public domain, I prefer not to draw attention to them by naming them, for reasons which you may come to appreciate. I was not altogether clear about what I hoped to find; but perhaps some detail of these localities not recorded by Forbes might associate with features of places described by Balmain, thus establishing a tentative link between the two narratives. So I headed for the Highland loch of the F story, the scene of the publicly established infanticide.

It was a September evening when I arrived, rather heavy and midgy. I dropped into a pub at the head of the loch for some food, and, getting into conversation with a couple of locals who were obviously not recent incomers, steered the conversation round to the subject of the murder. It was still well remembered the best part of twenty years later, and with predictable outrage and disgust. My informants could add little to what I already knew, but they did tell me that the scene of the crime was a few miles further down the loch, and gave me a number of details to help me identify it. My first thought was to visit the spot immediately, but the light was already fading and I thought it wiser to find accommodation for the night and leave my investigations for the morrow.

Around what I judged to be about a mile short of my objective I found an attractive-enough house with a B&B sign, stopped and rang the bell. It was answered by a pleasant middle-aged man who told me that unfortunately there were no vacancies, and I would not find anything else until I reached a village about fifteen miles further on. I looked downcast, I suppose, as I explained that I had something to do in the immediate vicinity the following morning. The man seemed to hesitate, looked at the ground briefly, and then said in a strange, shy manner:

'Well, we do have a cottage about a mile from here . . . It's a bit plain, but quite clean and all that. You could use that if you liked, the beds are all made up. You might find it a bit lonely, though?'

'Oh, I wouldn't mind that,' I said. 'I'm used to being on my own.'

The man nodded, still looking a shade hesitant, then seemed to dismiss his misgivings.

'Right then, I'll get the car out and you can follow me there.'

At the end of about a mile we turned right where there was an old wooden sign reading *Tom na Croiche*, on the opposite side of the road from the loch (I judged we must be very near the locality I was seeking), and drove a hundred yards or so up a rough track to a small wooden cottage with a rust-coloured corrugated-iron roof. It was rather overhung by trees, and bushes pushed towards the front door. A little behind the cottage and to the left stood a ruin which looked as if it might once have been a small chapel. Not far back from these remains there was a rather steep, thickly wooded knoll. Something about the place made me at once uneasy.

The man showed me over the cottage, which, as he had said, was small, plain and clean. There was a bedroom to the right of the front door, with two single beds, a chest of drawers and an old wardrobe. On the left was a sparsely furnished sitting room with a tiny kitchen off it, from which the back door with its huge rusty key opened towards the ruin. Opposite the front door a very steep straight stair led to a low-ceilinged upper floor, with on one side a small bathroom containing an old-fashioned zinc tub, on the other a door which I later found to be locked. The room with the locked door was above the bedroom in which I was to sleep.

The man suggested that if I wanted to pay him on the spot it would save me doubling back the following day – I could leave the key in the outside letter-box. I already knew that I very much did not want to spend the night alone in this house, but the human reluctance to lose face is an extraordinarily powerful motivation for resisting our deepest fears. I had told the man that I didn't mind being alone, and I would appear a fool if I now made some excuse not to stay here. So I paid him what was owed and thanked him for his kindness in making this decent little cottage available to me. As he made to go I felt the most awful urge to detain him, on any pretext at all, to keep him talking until I could think of some way of extracting myself, of going back on my decision to remain by myself in the house. But I did not do so.

When he had gone, and I was left alone, I told myself that I had to get a grip. What exactly was wrong? Nothing that I could possibly define. One would have to resort to some such formula as 'numinous dread', a subjective impression quite devoid of specific content. Feeling it best to confront my fear, I decided to go out the back and have a look at the chapel. Here the sinister atmosphere was, if anything, stronger. It was by now almost dark, but I could still see a little. The ruin was much like many another. The general structure suggested a chapel, but I was not enough of an architectural historian to be sure. In one corner was a short, truncated staircase – just a few steps. The interior was deep in thick, damp grass and rife with fungi; rowan and alder clung opportunistically to clefts between the collapsing stonework. The air was torpid and still, the silence absolute. I would have been delighted to have heard an owl hoot. Behind the ruin rose the knoll – thickly, silently watching. I knew I could not stay there, and so I retreated indoors. Once back in the house I said in my heart, 'How can I spend the night here and hope to emerge sane?' I felt that some ultimate, irreparable evil was about to come upon me.

I know I could have got into the car and driven off, and I probably should have done so. But a strange confusion was already overtaking my mind. There suddenly came into my head the conviction, 'This is where Torquil and Abigail killed the baby.' Then I remembered that this locality was the scene of Forbes's story, not Balmain's, and that *that* murder was committed not in a house but by the lochside. But I grasped this fact, as it were, with only one part of my mind; the other clung to my powerful impression. I was becoming confused between the two similar stories, unable to separate them in my consciousness, though I strove to do so. I felt that my brain was not working as it should. I began to feel feverish, almost in the grip of a kind of lucid delirium.

I went into the bedroom and sat down in an armchair, trying to sort out my ideas. I could not rid myself of the conviction that fate had drawn me to a place pervaded with evil. I stood up, paced up and down, sat down once more. Suddenly a vivid picture formed itself before my inner eye: a station on a railway line resembling the West Highland, by the sea, amid extravagant mountain scenery; the platform was sloping towards the shore, like a ferry ramp; along it walked a man with a tiny body and a huge head, the body itself diminishing proportionately in size from broad shoulder to almost invisible feet: the head was not ugly or misshapen, but serene and beautiful. I knew I had seen this somewhere before, but I couldn't decide whether in reality or in dream; the more I struggled to sort this out in my head, the more confused and frightened I became. The picture was dissolving and giving place to another scene: a crowded street in some Mediterranean town. I had been there, or experienced it – had I known it or dreamt it? Was I dreaming now? No, I appeared to be awake, I could see all the features of the room quite clearly in the weak electric light. And so it went on. New images continued to emerge from somewhere, not flashingly, but with a slow insidious deliberation. The horror lay not in the images themselves – some indeed were frightening, yet others were quite normal, even mundane – but rather in my inability to place them, to remember where I knew them from, to control them or find in them any meaningful order. They seemed neither dreams I had had nor events I had experienced – yet I knew them, recognized them all! How could this be?

This went on for a very long time. Sometimes there were respites, when the images receded for a time and I sat on, dazed and confused, unable to stir myself, dreading their return. And return they did, again and again, incalculably many of them, memories that were fearful because they seemed to arise from no remembered source. Finally there arose an image different from the others in that it seemed to manifest itself not to my inner vision, but almost – I say 'almost' because I am not quite sure of it – to my physical eye. It consisted in an apparition which appeared to descend through the ceiling, a vague, hooded male figure like an executioner, staring at me through eye-slits. I knew somehow that his name was Kaprick Harpmusic. He did not speak, but in some way I couldn't and can't grasp he communicated to me, imprinted his thought directly on my consciousness; and his word was this:

'You do not exist! You have no reality!'

Even as I received this, the last vestiges of my personality seemed to dissolve and I believe I lost consciousness. When I came to, I'm not sure how much later, dawn was breaking. The sickening flow of images had gone and though I was exhausted my mind was clear. The atmosphere of numinous terror no longer clung to my surroundings. And I understood, without any shadow of doubting, what I had undergone during the night. All those images which I remembered as experiences, but which I knew I had neither lived nor dreamt, had been experienced by others. Yes, I had been remembering other people's experiences! Which meant that there was in reality no 'individual' experience; consciousness does not belong to me or to you, but is a common possession which is somehow, as it were, divided up between us. The filter of my brain, which should have excluded the experience of 'others', had temporarily broken down and I had been overwhelmed by the ingress of what would, in the conventional understanding, be regarded as alien memory, memory not my own. But if we all, potentially, have access to all experience, in what sense can it be said that we individually exist? My personality had been destroyed – executed – during the course of that fearful night, and if it now appeared to have been recovered, reassembled, it seemed to me that it was in a phantom form.

After a couple of hours of deep sleep I rose, washed and left Tom na Croiche. I had abandoned my intention of investigating the matter of the twin infanticides at points further north. What could I possibly hope to make of it all, in the face of the new insights which I had unwillingly received? Might it be that the events of the infanticide at this place had imprinted themselves upon Balmain's consciousness, in the same way as those alien images had come to me, and that his conscious mind had then made of them a new, although related reality? A new event in time? I could not tell. It seemed to me now that our relationship to *that which is* (what I am shy of calling God) – to that, I mean, which underlies and indwells the whole and from which the whole derives – is like that of characters to their author. We have only a dependent, relative kind of reality, one which serves us for the present. If we have more substance than fictional characters it is only because we are a little higher up than they on the scale of diminishing reality. This is no new idea, of course, but through my experiences that night at Tom na Croiche I felt I had apprehended its truth directly.

I retraced my steps and stopped at the inn of the previous night to get some breakfast. As I was leaving I said to the landlord, as casually as I could manage:

'I noticed a sign a few miles up the road to a house called Tom na Croiche. I'm trying to pick up a bit of Gaelic, and I couldn't place the last word – can you tell me what it means?'

He gave me that same stealthy, guarded kind of look

that I had encountered the previous night on the face of the owner of the cottage.

'*Tom na Croiche,*' he replied. 'It means the knoll of the gibbet, the knoll of the gallows. It's generally known in English as *The Hangman's Knowe*. That wee hill behind the house is where public executions took place in past days. The last public hanging was in 1680.'

Well, I went home and took up my normal life again, and gradually these impressions were effaced from the forefront of my consciousness. But they remain there at the back of my mind, to haunt and to trouble me. I'll never feel quite the same again about my 'self', never pronounce with the confidence of old on the nature of what I used to think of as my identity. Yet here I am, sitting at this entirely solid table with my pen in my hand. I have told you the story of this strange experience of mine. Judge yourself, reader, of my reality.

Searching for words,
Hunting for phrases,
When will it end?
Esteeming knowledge
And gathering information
Only maddens the spirit.
Just entrust yourself
To your own nature,
Empty and illuminating.
Beyond this,
I have nothing to teach.

Bankei Yotaku, 1622–93